FOLLOWING THE *RAINBOW*

Jody followed Lauren's pointing finger. Something was moving out there in the water . . . dark, gleaming bodies . . . was it a group of dolphins? Then she saw the unmistakeable shape of tail fins rising into the air and slapping down hard against the water, sending up a fan of spray. It was the distinctive whale behavior known as lob-tailing.

As Jody watched in silent wonder, she heard the pod respond to the cries of Seb and Tía. The faintly eerie sound of their voices drifted inland, making her shiver.

"There must be twenty of them at least!" Gavin Davis said softly.

"Seb family!" Hal cried. A rare smile lit his face. "Seb and Tía not lonely no more."

Look out for more titles in this series

1. Into the Blue
2. Touching the Waves
3. Riding the Storm
4. Under the Stars
5. Chasing the Dream
6. Racing the Wind

Dolphin Diaries™

Ben M. Baglio

Illustrations by Judith Lawton

FOLLOWING THE *RAINBOW*

AN
APPLE
PAPERBACK

SCHOLASTIC INC.
New York Toronto London Auckland Sydney
Mexico City New Delhi Hong Kong Buenos Aires

No part of this publication may be reproduced in whole or in part, or stored in a retrieval system, or transmitted in any form or by any means, electronic, mechanical, photocopying, recording, or otherwise, without written permission of the publisher. For information regarding permission, write to Working Partners Limited, 1 Albion Place, London W6 OQT, United Kingdom.

ISBN 0-439-44614-7

Text copyright © 2001 by Working Partners Limited.
Illustrations copyright © 2001 by Judith Lawton.

All rights reserved. Published by Scholastic Inc., 557 Broadway,
New York, NY 10012, by arrangement with Working Partners Limited.
DOLPHIN DIARIES is a trademark of Working Partners Limited.
SCHOLASTIC, APPLE PAPERBACKS, and associated logos are trademarks
and/or registered trademarks of Scholastic Inc.

12 11 10 9 8 7 6   3 4 5 6 7/0

Printed in the U.S.A.   40
First Scholastic printing, September 2002

Special thanks to Lisa Tuttle

Thanks also to the Whale and Dolphin
Conservation Society for reviewing the
information contained in this book

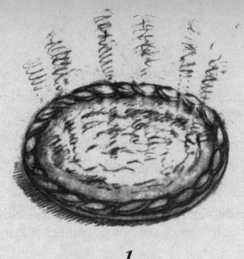

1

November 22 — midmorning — Thanksgiving — Caracas, Venezuela
My mouth is watering. Even sitting out on deck I can smell pumpkin pie and roast turkey. Our Thanksgiving dinner is going to be delicious.

This harbor is so busy! We're still trying to find a place to moor. I wonder what time we'll have dinner. I'm starving already. . . .

Jody broke off. She shook her head ruefully. She'd decided to write in her diary to take her mind off her rumbling stomach, and what did she write about? Food! Jody didn't think she would see any dolphins today in this noisy harbor, so crowded with boats of all sizes. Still, she took another look out at the murky water, just in case. Maybe she would catch sight of some bottlenose dolphins or harbor porpoises playing among the traffic. . . .

Jody loved dolphins more than anything. She hoped to become a marine biologist someday like her parents, Craig and Gina McGrath. Her whole family had been living on board their boat, *Dolphin Dreamer,* since June, conducting a scientific project called Dolphin Universe. They had traveled from their home in Florida, via the Bahamas, down to South America, studying dolphins in the wild and making contact with other scientists along the way.

It was a dream come true for Jody, and she wouldn't have changed places with anyone in the world. But even so, there were times when living on a boat had its drawbacks. It was hard to escape from her annoying younger brothers, Jimmy and Sean. Her cabin mate, Brittany Pierce — whose dad, Harry, was the boat's captain — wasn't always easy to get along with. And when Jody felt bored and restless, as she did now, there was nowhere to go.

But Jody was not the type to sit around and mope. Noticing her mom and dad standing by the railing on the lower deck, she clambered down from her perch on the forward deck and joined them.

Her dad turned and smiled at her. "I thought you'd be helping Mei Lin with the cooking," he said. Mei Lin was the cook and engineer on *Dolphin Dreamer*.

Jody shook her head. "Brittany got there first. Mei Lin says there's barely enough room for two in the galley," she explained.

"That's true enough," Jody's mother agreed. Tucking a strand of dark hair behind her ear, she added, "I'll have to chase both Mei Lin and Brittany out while I make my Sweet Potato Surprise — I need elbow room when I cook!"

Jody frowned anxiously. "You haven't made your special dish yet?" she asked. "Aren't you leaving it until the last minute?"

"Sorry, sweetie, but I'm missing a couple of vital ingredients. As soon as we've docked, I'll rush out and buy them," Gina explained. "We'll just have to eat a little later than usual, that's all," she added.

Jody groaned and rolled her eyes theatrically. "But I'm starving!"

"It'll be worth the wait," Craig said, grinning. He put one arm around his wife and one around his daughter. "It wouldn't be Thanksgiving without your mother's Sweet Potato Surprise!"

Jody sighed. She had to admit it was a family tradition and, hungry as she was, it *would* be worth the wait. She just had to keep her mind off her stomach. "How long will we stay in Caracas?" she asked.

"About a week," her father replied. "We've got several meetings scheduled with some local scientists, and while we're tied up here, Harry can see to a few minor repairs."

"Don't worry, the week after that will be more exciting," Gina put in. "We're going to sail up to Curaçao and Bonaire before we head for the Panama Canal. The diving is supposed to be great off Bonaire," she added, giving Jody a smile.

Jody grinned back. Then she thought of something that might distract her from her rumbling stomach.

"I'll go and check my e-mail," she said. Jody and the rest of the crew on board *Dolphin Dreamer* made the most of using e-mail when they were docked: Unless it was important, they didn't make phone calls or go on-line while at sea, because that meant using an expensive satellite link.

"Sure, go ahead," her dad replied.

Jody hurried down below. Brittany was still in the galley helping Mei Lin. In the saloon her brothers were busy constructing a centerpiece for the table. Jody remembered that Maddie had suggested the boys could make a few decorative paper turkeys. Maddie was their onboard teacher, as well as her parents' assistant. However, mere turkeys were not exciting enough for the eight-year-old twins. Jody saw that Sean was cutting out grim-faced Pilgrims armed with enormous muskets, while Jimmy colored in a line of fierce, ax-wielding Native Americans.

Jody paused. "Hey, guys, the Indians didn't fight with the Pilgrims," she pointed out. "They brought them food and helped them survive the harsh winter. Remember? The first Thanksgiving was all about friendship!"

Sean sighed. "We know that. But they weren't so friendly to the turkeys, were they?"

"They're going on a *biiiig* turkey hunt," Jimmy explained.

Jody shrugged and headed for the door, calling over her shoulder, "Just leave some room on the table for food, would you?"

Alone in her cabin, Jody settled down with her laptop and logged on. She smiled happily as messages popped up in her mailbox. There were two from Lindsay, her best friend back home, and four from other school friends, plus the monthly school newsletter. Even her grandpa had finally caught on to modern technology and forwarded a bunch of jokes. Then Jody noticed with surprise that she had three e-mails from Lauren Rozakis.

Lauren lived in the Florida Keys. Her parents ran a dolphin-therapy center called CETA, which had been the first port of call for *Dolphin Dreamer*. Jody and

Lauren had become friends and had decided to keep in touch — but three e-mails in one week was far more than usual! Puzzled, Jody opened the first.

Hey, Jody, remember Hal Davis, the little boy who was helped by Rosie?

Jody grinned. "How could I forget?" she murmured. Rosie was the youngest of the dolphins owned by Lauren's parents. At their therapy center, the dolphins were the "teachers" that helped children with learning difficulties. Jody remembered how much the little boy had loved Rosie. Hal was autistic, which meant he found it hard to communicate with people. His wealthy parents had tried everything to help him, but nothing seemed to work. Then, thanks to an accidental meeting with Jody, Lauren, and Brittany, they had agreed to bring him to CETA. Hal had been fascinated by the dolphins, and Rosie had been able to reach him as no human teacher could. Wondering how the little boy was doing, Jody continued reading:

Hal's parents have invited my family to join them for an all-expenses-paid week in the Canary Islands! My teacher has said the trip will be educational so it is OK for me to miss a week of school. We're flying out there right after Thanksgiving.

I'm so excited! Dad always has to work, so this will be our first family vacation in five years, and my first time ever outside America! I have been reading up on the Canary Islands — they are near Africa, in case you don't know — and the sea there is full of different kinds of whales and dolphins. I can't wait to see them!

Jody was pleased for Lauren but she couldn't help feeling a little envious. For her, the next week promised to be rather dull, with nothing but the usual routine of schoolwork with Maddie while her parents went to meetings and Harry worked on the boat. She opened Lauren's second message.

Disaster! The marine specialist who was going to keep CETA open while we're away has gotten pneu-

monia and can't come. There's nobody else my folks trust to do it, so the vacation is off. And I was so looking forward to it!

"Oh, no!" Jody cried sympathetically, just as the cabin door opened.

"What's wrong?" asked Brittany, coming in.

Jody quickly explained about Lauren.

Brittany frowned. "Just because her parents want to stay home doesn't mean *she* has to. Why don't they let Lauren go on her own?"

Jody shrugged. Then she remembered she had a third e-mail from Lauren. She clicked it open and began to read, then stopped, her mouth dropping open in disbelief.

"What?" Brittany demanded.

Jody read Lauren's letter aloud:

Gavin Davis is a hero! Even though Mom and Dad can't make it, he still wants me to come. And not on my own. He's offered to pay for you and Brittany to come, too!

Brittany gasped.

Breathlessly, Jody read on:

He's promised to sort out all the travel arrangements. I'm leaving on Saturday. I hope he can talk your folks into letting you go! The three of us would have such a great time! Fingers crossed, I'll see you in Madrid on Saturday night! I can't believe it!

Brittany gave a yelp of excitement, but Jody frowned. Surely Lauren didn't mean the day after tomorrow?

With a funny feeling in her stomach, she checked the date of Lauren's e-mail. November the twentieth. Two days ago.

"Hang on, Brit," she said uneasily. "Lauren wrote this two days ago, and we still haven't heard from Mr. Davis. Lauren's going on Saturday the twenty-fourth. That's the day after tomorrow. If he really wanted us to come he would have invited us by now."

Brittany shook her head, smiling confidently. "We've been at sea, remember? So Mr. Davis couldn't get through before today. I bet he sent an e-mail to your parents." She wrapped her arms around herself and exclaimed, "Oh, I can't wait!"

Jody bit her lip and said nothing. She was usually optimistic, but surely this was too good to be true.

Brittany frowned. "What's wrong? Don't you *want* to go?"

"Yes, sure I do, but . . ." Jody shook her head. "Well, I don't think we'll be allowed."

Britt just can't wait to go. . . .

"Why not?" Brittany looked determined. "It won't cost our folks anything — Gavin Davis has offered to pay for it all! He can afford it, he's a millionaire! And if Lauren's teacher is letting her miss school, Maddie can do the same for us." She folded her arms and raised her eyebrows. "I don't know about your parents, but I can't think of one good reason for my dad to say no!"

"Well, I can," Jody said. Wary of setting off one of Brittany's temper tantrums, she spoke gently. "*Dolphin Dreamer* has a schedule to keep, you know. Mom and Dad want to leave Caracas in a week. If you and I went to the Canary Islands, we wouldn't be back by then."

To Jody's relief, Brittany didn't explode. She could be short-tempered and selfish, but she had calmed down a lot over the past few months. Now she spoke in a reasonable voice. "Maybe they wouldn't mind staying just an extra couple of days. Or maybe we could come back earlier than Lauren," she suggested. "Anyway, the least we can do is ask!"

Jody thought about this, unable to stop a flicker of excitement. "You're right!" she agreed. She jumped up, and the two girls hurried off in search of Craig, Gina, and Harry.

They weren't in their cabins, and when Jody and Brittany looked into the saloon there was only Maddie helping Sean and Jimmy with their table display.

When they reached the deck it was deserted, except for first mate Cameron Tucker, who was checking that the ropes that tied them to the dock were secure.

"Where's my dad?" Brittany asked impatiently.

Cam turned and smiled at them. "Harry went to see the harbormaster and arrange for our stay here," he explained. "Craig went with him — there's always a lot of paperwork to deal with, so it can take some time."

"What about Mom?" Jody asked. "Where's she?"

"She went shopping," Cam replied. "Just left a couple of minutes ago. Something about Sweet Potato Surprise?" Cam cocked his head quizzically as both girls groaned in dismay. "Don't you like sweet potatoes?" he asked, sounding puzzled.

"It's not that," Jody explained. "It's just that we need to talk to her or Dad *urgently*!"

Cam shrugged. "Sorry. Can I help? No? Well, guess you'll have to wait."

The next hour dragged by. Jody couldn't concentrate on anything. She and Brittany kept popping up on deck like jack-in-the-boxes until, finally, Gina appeared, carrying bags of groceries.

"Mom!" Jody gasped as soon as her mother was on board. "Have you heard from Gavin Davis?"

Her mother looked at her blankly.

"The millionaire businessman we met at CETA," Brittany reminded her. "Hal's father."

"Oh, yes, I remember," Gina replied. She shook her head. "No, why would I?" She handed a bag to Jody. "Here, help me get these below, please. I need to start cooking."

"Please, could you check your e-mails first?" Jody begged.

Gina gave her a puzzled look. "I thought you were hungry."

"I am, but this is more important than food," Jody said.

"*Much* more," Brittany chimed in.

Gina laughed. "Now you've got me curious! OK, I'll check my e-mails right away. Want to tell me what this is all about?"

The two girls followed her below, and Jody quickly explained.

Sure enough, when Gina logged on, she found a long message from Gavin Davis. "Hmmm," she said, reading quickly. "Looks like he's been spending quite a lot of time trying to reach us!"

"What does he say?" Jody asked.

"Well, like you said, he's inviting you and Brittany to La Gomera in the Canary Islands," Gina replied. "It's very short notice . . . and such a long way to go . . . just the two of you . . . don't know . . ." She sounded doubtful, and Jody's heart sank.

"On the other hand," Gina went on, "it does fit in with our schedule, and Gavin has gone to an awful lot of trouble. Sounds like you girls really impressed the Davises, if they think their little boy won't enjoy this vacation without you. What a pity Sean and Jimmy don't feel the same way!" She grinned mischievously at the two girls.

Brittany caught her breath with excitement.

Jody grinned back at her mom, feeling butterflies in her stomach. "So, we *can* go?"

"I didn't say that," her mother replied quickly. "But I'll think about it. And I'm not agreeing to anything before I talk with your dad — and Harry," she added, with a nod at Brittany.

"Can I read what Mr. Davis said?" Jody asked.

"Go ahead." Her mother gestured at the screen. Jody leaned over her shoulder and quickly scanned the letter.

. . . Of course, I want to talk to you personally before making any travel arrangements, but since you've been unreachable, and time is so short, I hope you won't mind that I've checked on flight availability. Alice and Jerry Rozakis reminded me that I could find your schedule posted on the Dolphin Universe web site. So I've tried to work out some travel arrangements that seem to fit into your schedule. If they don't, just say so!

I can book seats for Jody and Brittany to fly out of Caracas on Saturday morning, and return either the following Saturday, or on Friday, if that would be better. Going out, there are seats available on the early morning flight to Madrid, which arrives only half an hour after Lauren's flight from Miami. My wife and I are meeting Lauren in Madrid, and we fly to Tenerife early Sunday morning. From there we'll take the ferry to the island of La Gomera, where we've rented a villa.

It would make such a difference to Lauren, to Hal, and to us to have Jody and Brittany along! Hal often asks when he can see the girls again. I know they would make this vacation really extra special for him if they come. Janet and I have always felt that they were every bit as important as the dolphins at CETA in breaking through Hal's "shell" — and we'd really like to do something to show our thanks.

I hope you'll agree. Please think about it. Call me when you've decided. If I haven't heard from you by then, I'll try to call again on Thanksgiving.

At that moment, right on cue, Gina's cell phone began to ring.

2

November 24 — almost midnight! — Madrid, Spain
Wow, this has all happened so fast that I can still hardly
believe we're really here!

Brittany and I flew out of the Caracas airport — was it
only this morning? Now we are half a world away, in
Spain. Mr. and Mrs. Davis met us at the airport in Madrid.
Lauren was with them, and I couldn't believe my eyes
when I saw her — her arm's in a cast! She fell off her bike
and broke her arm more than a week ago, but she was so
excited about this trip that she never even thought to
mention it in her e-mails to me and Brittany. She won't be

18

able to go swimming while we're here, but she says she doesn't mind too much — after all, she can swim with dolphins all year-round at home!

Mr. Davis was looking very sharp as he'd just finished some business in Madrid. We haven't seen Hal yet — it was past his bedtime, so he stayed at the hotel with his nanny (we haven't met her yet, either).

Now we're in our hotel room. Lauren and Britt are laughing at some old American show dubbed in Spanish on the TV.

Uh-oh . . . that was Mrs. Davis at the door. She told us to get some sleep. We have to get up in just a few hours to catch the plane to Tenerife!

Jody felt as if she hadn't slept for more than ten minutes when she was jolted awake by the shrill ring of a telephone. She heard Brittany groaning and Lauren yawning as she stumbled out of bed and went in search of her clothes.

There was no time for breakfast. The Davises bundled them into a cab in the darkness outside the hotel, promising they could get something to eat at the airport.

Soon they were settled in the departure lounge, sipping from cups of hot chocolate and munching pastries as they waited for their flight to be called.

Hal was a bundle of unstoppable energy. He acted as if he didn't remember Lauren, Jody, and Brittany. He didn't respond when they spoke to him and barely even looked at them, showing far more interest in a trash can with a shiny silver lid he could flip in and out.

Jody watched as his nanny, Nicole Jenner, managed to distract the little boy, gently drawing his attention to the planes outside the big windows. Nicole was a fit, wiry young woman with lots of curly red hair, bright blue eyes, and a quick smile.

"We're really lucky to have found Nicole," Gavin Davis commented quietly. "She seems to understand how Hal's mind works. Even better, he likes her. He responds to her the way he does to you girls."

"Yes, well, he seemed to like us at CETA," Jody said, remembering how she and Lauren had taken Hal into the water to play with Rosie the dolphin. "But I don't think he remembers me."

"Oh, he remembers you, all right!" Janet Davis spoke up. "When we explained to Hal that Lauren and her mom and dad were coming on vacation with us, he started shouting, 'And Jody! And Brittany!' He was very determined," she finished, laughing.

"Hal doesn't always know how to express his feelings," Gavin Davis said. "But he certainly has them, locked inside. It was Rosie who gave us the first key to unlocking them."

Jody remembered the magical moment when Hal had met Rosie. It had been the first time she'd heard Hal speak, and the first time she'd seen him really respond to another living creature. "Will there be dolphins where we're going?" she asked.

"Honestly, talk about a one-track mind!" Brittany exclaimed. She made a face. "There are other things in the world besides dolphins, you know, Jody!"

Jody felt embarrassed. "I was thinking of Hal," she protested.

"So were we when we planned this vacation," Mr. Davis replied. He smiled, his kind gray eyes crinkling behind his round glasses. "There are lots of dolphins in the waters between Tenerife and La Gomera," he explained.

"And whales!" his wife put in.

"That's right," Mr. Davis agreed. "Hopefully, Hal will take to whales the way he's taken to dolphins. We thought a whale-watching tour would make a great vacation treat."

"Not only that, but we have friends who live on La Gomera," Janet Davis added. "We've been meaning to visit them for ages."

Jody was thrilled at the prospect of getting close to some whales. Lauren looked excited, too, she noticed. More surprisingly, so did Brittany.

"So, will we go out whale-watching on *Daisy Mae*?" Brittany asked eagerly.

Daisy Mae was the Davises' large, luxurious yacht. Jody remembered that Brittany had been especially impressed by it back in Florida.

Brittany's bright smile faded as Gavin and Janet Davis shook their heads.

"We left *Daisy Mae* back home. It would have taken

too long to travel here by sea," Gavin Davis explained. "I've chartered a boat with a captain and a local guide who know the area."

Janet Davis touched her husband's arm. "I think they're calling our flight," she said. "You'd better go round up Nicole and Hal."

After the long journey across the Atlantic the day before, the flight from Madrid to the Reina Sofia airport in Tenerife seemed to take no time at all. Soon after landing, the party split into two taxis and headed for the ferry terminal at Los Cristianos.

"There's no airport on La Gomera," Gavin Davis explained. "The only way to get there is by boat. That's why it hasn't become such a huge tourist trap like Tenerife. It's still very unspoiled. People who visit La Gomera are more interested in peace and quiet and getting close to nature."

Jody thought that sounded great. She gazed out the taxi window at the dry, barren landscape. Spiky cacti pushed up out of the gray, rocky soil. On one side of the road was the sparkling sea; on the other, a huge mountain loomed over them — a dramatic sight, especially with the faint icing of snow over the peak.

"What's that mountain?" Lauren asked.

"That's El Teide," Mr. Davis replied. "It's a dormant volcano. And it's enormous — we'll even be able to see it from La Gomera!"

The cabs soon arrived at Los Cristianos. Jody gazed at the small harbor packed with different types of boats — sailing yachts, fishing boats, pleasure cruisers, and tour boats. Signs in English, Spanish, and German advertised not only ferry services, but dolphin-watching tours, shark fishing, even a pirate adventure — her brothers would go for that one, she thought.

"There, that's the one," said Mr. Davis, leading the way toward a large, eye-catching sign that announced: REGULAR, SPEEDY SERVICE TO LA GOMERA — ON FOOT OR IN A CAR, WE'RE THE FASTEST BY FAR!

A teenage boy in a jacket with the ferry company's logo on the pocket was standing at the entrance for foot-passengers. Spotting Lauren's plaster cast, he darted forward. "Here, let me take that bag for you," he said in barely accented English.

Lauren looked embarrassed. "I'm OK, it's not heavy," she said, shaking her head.

"But you've only got one good arm," he pointed out reasonably. "You'll need to hold on to the railing as you go upstairs."

"Are we going upstairs?" Jody asked. She craned her neck to study the ferry that was moored beside them.

The boy turned to her. He had a good-looking, friendly face with large, dark, wide-set eyes. "The best views are from the upper deck," he said. "That's where I'd go, myself. But maybe you'd rather go inside to the passenger lounge or the café?"

"It's definitely the upper deck for me." Gavin Davis decided, heading for the stairs.

"Me, too," said Lauren, handing the boy her bag with a shy smile.

"Can you carry mine as well?" Brittany asked. "It's kind of bulky."

"Sure." He tucked Lauren's smaller bag under one arm and took hold of Brittany's overstuffed carryall, then looked at Jody again. "Room for one more." He smiled.

Jody shook her head. "Mine's a backpack," she pointed out, lifting her arms to show that she had both hands free.

"Traveling light," the boy commented. "Are you just going to La Gomera for the day?"

"No, all week," Jody told him as they followed the others toward the metal stairs.

"You're American?" he asked.

"Yes, from Florida." Then she asked curiously, "How about you?"

He laughed. "I'm a native-born Gomero! What else did you think?"

"I don't know," Jody confessed. "But your English is so good, I wondered . . ."

"My mother is English," he explained, climbing the stairs. "So even though my father is Spanish, we usually speak English at home."

They had reached the top deck. There were lots of benches there, many of them already filled with other passengers. The boy stowed Lauren's and Brittany's bags beneath an unoccupied seat. "From here you'll have the best view of La Gomera as we approach," he promised.

"Will we see any dolphins or whales?" Jody asked.

The boy's face lit up. "Oh, yes! There are usually dolphins in the harbor. The whales prefer deeper water. It gets very deep in the channel between Tenerife and La Gomera, so there are always whales there." His thick brown bangs flopped into his eyes as he spoke, and he brushed them back impatiently. "Pilot whales live here year-round," he went on, warming to the subject. "There

Meeting Mario for the first time!

are about five hundred of them living in these waters. Also, some kinds of beaked whales. But the whales that migrate, like the sperm whales, also pass through on their journeys, so you might see them. They're massive!"

"You seem to know a lot about whales," Brittany commented dryly.

He shrugged his shoulders and laughed. "I'm sorry if I'm boring you. . . ."

"Oh, no!" Jody exclaimed quickly. "We love whales — and dolphins, too! My parents are marine biologists, specializing in dolphins, and Lauren's —"

The boy's eyes widened. "Really!" he interrupted. "That's amazing!" Moving toward Gavin Davis, the boy said eagerly, "I'd love to hear about your work, sir! How you got started and where you studied — if you could —"

Mr. Davis had been chatting quietly to his wife, not paying attention to the conversation about whales. He looked bewildered by the boy's excitement.

"Oh, no, that's not my father," Jody said quickly, realizing the mistake. "I'm sorry, I should have explained!

Our parents aren't here. We came with friends. This is Gavin Davis."

Automatically, Mr. Davis put out his hand. "Pleased to meet you."

"Mario Gomez," said the boy, shaking hands. He looked embarrassed.

Trying to smooth over the awkwardness, Jody quickly introduced herself and the others.

"It was nice meeting you," Mario said. "I hope you'll enjoy the journey." He began to move away.

"Oh, please, can't you stay?" Jody burst out impulsively. "I'd really like to hear more about the whales and dolphins."

"So would I," Lauren chimed in.

At that, Mario relaxed. He smiled shyly. "And maybe you could tell me some more about what your parents do?"

Jody and Lauren nodded vigorously.

"*My* dad is a boat captain," Brittany said, not to be left out.

Mario smiled at her. "That's a good job, too. And speaking of jobs, I'd better get back to mine," he said.

"I'll come and talk to you some more once we're under way," he promised.

Brittany gazed after Mario as he hurried away. "He's not stuck-up at all," she said approvingly.

Jody was surprised. "Why would he be?"

"In my experience, boys that good-looking are usually very conceited," Brittany said in a worldly wise tone. "Mario acts like he doesn't even *know* how cute he is!"

Jody felt a little irritated with Brittany. Sure, Mario was cute, but he was also friendly and obviously as enthusiastic about whales and dolphins as Jody — that was the attraction for her.

She turned away to look out at the harbor. Her eyes scanned the shining water, searching for movement. Then she caught her breath at the sight that was always so magical to her — the beautiful curving body of a dolphin leaping out of the water. As it vanished again with hardly a splash, Jody saw that it wasn't alone. Two other sleek gray animals were swimming alongside, playfully rolling and swooping under the surface. From this distance Jody couldn't tell if they were bottlenose or common dolphins, or perhaps some kind she hadn't encountered yet.

Jody glanced around, wanting to share the sight. Then Nicole appeared, dragging a reluctant, struggling Hal. "Come on, Hal," she said firmly. "We have to stay together. No more running off!"

"Hal, look, dolphins!" Jody called to the little boy.

It was the magic word. Hal rushed to join Jody at the railing. So did a dozen other passengers, all attracted by the mention of dolphins.

The trio of playful dolphins swam closer to the ferry, as if they knew they had an audience. They began leaping into the air, trying to outdo one another. Their streamlined gray bodies gleamed in the sunshine, and the sea spray sparkled with a thousand tiny rainbows.

Jody glanced at Hal. A look of peace spread across the boy's troubled face as he gazed steadily at the frolicking dolphins.

All too soon, the dolphins moved on, chasing one another out of sight into deeper water.

At the same time, a deep, noisy rumble from below

told Jody that the ferry was moving. They pulled away from the dock and headed toward the open sea. Hal seemed to find the noise and movement soothing and didn't fuss about the dolphins' disappearance.

The ferry journey was much faster and bumpier than Jody had expected. The wind whipped her hair around her face as she clung to the railing and stared out to sea. Most of the other passengers went back to their seats.

"I'm going for a walk," Brittany announced. "Anybody want to come with me?"

"I will," Lauren decided.

"If you find the café, would you be able to get us some sodas?" asked Janet Davis, digging into her purse.

Jody went on scanning the ocean. A few minutes later, someone came to the railing beside her. She looked up, expecting Lauren, and was surprised to see Mario instead. "I haven't seen any whales yet," she told him. "Am I looking in the wrong place?"

Mario smiled. "Whales aren't that easy to spot," he replied, pushing back his unruly hair. "They spend nearly their whole lives underwater — they don't leap into the air the way dolphins do."

Jody smiled back at him. "So how do you get to see the whales?" she persisted.

"You have to be lucky," Mario told her. "It takes time and patience. And it helps if you've seen them before and know what you're looking at — otherwise, you might not recognize them. You have to get very close, really. A smaller boat than this is better for whale watching . . . and this ferry goes far too fast." A shadow seemed to pass across his face, and he frowned.

"It doesn't matter if I don't see any whales today," Jody told him, in case he was worried she'd be disappointed. "Mr. Davis has rented a boat to take us all out whale watching from La Gomera."

Mario nodded, but it seemed to Jody that he still looked unhappy about something. She was wondering how to ask when he said briskly, "You were going to tell me about your parents. Do they study dolphins all the time? Is that really their job? How does that work?"

Jody began to explain about Dolphin Universe and her life on board *Dolphin Dreamer*. Mario was interested in every detail. Whenever she stopped for breath he had a dozen questions to ask. The time flew by as they talked, and they were both startled to find that they'd reached the island of La Gomera, and it was time to disembark.

Mario retrieved a toy that Hal had dropped and carried Lauren's and Brittany's bags downstairs. He refused the tip that Mr. Davis tried to give him and shook everyone's hands as he wished them well. "Enjoy your stay on La Gomera," he said warmly. "I hope you see lots of whales, Jody!"

Jody smiled back. It seemed strange to be saying goodbye. Already, Mario felt like an old friend. "I'll tell you all about it next weekend on the way back," she said.

"I'll look for you then," he promised.

The Davises had hired a car for the vacation, which was waiting for them on the dock. It was a big minivan, with sliding doors, three rows of seats, and more than enough room for all their luggage.

Jody gazed eagerly out the window. La Gomera was much smaller than Tenerife, but it, too, was dry and rocky. However, as they headed farther inland, the desert-like appearance changed. There were bright splashes of green on the bare slopes, and as they traveled higher into the mountainous interior, Jody saw that the steep hillsides had been shaped into terraces for farming. There were lots of leafy palm trees, and she also recognized banana and avocado plants.

Eventually, Gavin Davis steered the car off the main road onto a driveway lined with towering palms. At the end of the driveway was a large white villa with an orange-tiled roof. It was two stories high and very long, but despite its size it wasn't fancy — quite plain, and as friendly and homely looking as the smaller houses in the villages they had passed through. The walls were coarsely plastered, and the big wooden shutters framing each big window had been painted a fresh, bright pink.

While Mr. Davis unpacked the car, the girls followed Mrs. Davis inside, through a cool, stone-floored entrance hall, then upstairs and along a hallway where ceiling fans twirled and whispered softly.

"I hope you don't mind sharing a room," Janet Davis said, opening a door. "There were three beds in this one, and I thought it would be more fun than splitting you up. There's your own bathroom through there."

35

They chorused their thanks. To Jody, the spacious room looked positively palatial after the tiny cabin she'd been used to sharing with Brittany!

"I'll leave you girls to get settled in," Mrs. Davis went on. "I'm just going back to the kitchen to introduce myself to the cook. She's called Diamantina — a friend of Gavin's recommended her. Oh, and Nicole wants to talk to you about your study plans."

As soon as the door closed behind Mrs. Davis, Brittany frowned. "What study plans?"

This was news to Jody, too, but Lauren nodded. "Oh, yeah. To keep my teacher happy about me missing school, I promised I'd do a special project while I was here. My mom was going to supervise — when she couldn't come, Mr. Davis said Hal's nanny would help."

Brittany looked stubborn, her jaw thrust forward. "Well, she'd better not try to make *me* do any work!" she said fiercely. "Nobody's going to boss me around! You two can do what you like, but I came here for a fun vacation — and that's exactly what I'm going to have!"

3

Jody stared at Brittany in dismay. There was a knock at the door, and then Nicole looked in. "Can I talk to you?" she asked.

Jody's heart sank. What timing! Brittany was sure to make trouble.

Nicole came in. She had a canvas bag slung over one shoulder. "I wanted to talk to Lauren about our study plan for the week," she explained. Then she turned to Jody and Brittany and smiled. "But I don't think you two should be left out. Having something to focus on will help you all get even more out of this week abroad.

I'm sure your teacher will be pleased, too," she added. "So, I'd like you each to decide on a subject and present a report by the end of the week."

"What sort of subject?" Lauren asked, jumping in before Brittany could say anything.

"Something with a local connection," Nicole replied. "It could be history, or local lifestyles, or maybe the plants or wildlife, or —"

"Dolphins?" Jody asked hopefully.

Brittany snorted disdainfully.

Nicole shook her head, smiling teasingly. "*Not* the bottlenose dolphin! From what I've heard, you already know enough on that subject to write a book!"

Jody grinned, feeling her cheeks heat up.

"I've got some ideas if you need them," Nicole said encouragingly.

"Thanks," said Jody. She liked Nicole and felt sure anything she suggested would be fun, not really like work at all.

"Well, Brittany, what do you think?" Nicole asked, turning to the other girl.

"I think it sounds stupid," Brittany snapped. She tossed

her long blond hair. "I don't mind practicing my Spanish while I'm here, but I am not going to write a stupid report!" She glared at Nicole. "And you can't make me!"

Nicole looked surprised. "Who said anything about *writing* a report?" Digging into her shoulder bag, she pulled out a compact, state-of-the-art camcorder. "I thought multimedia would be more interesting," she went on, "so Mr. Davis provided this. We've got the software for editing and adding all sorts of neat stuff to the finished film — still pictures, animation, a sound track, you name it."

Brittany looked stunned. Her mouth dropped open.

"Cool," Lauren murmured, her gray eyes sparkling with excitement.

"The only problem is," Nicole said slowly, "although we've got three computers here, there's only the one camcorder, so you'll have to take turns —"

"That sounds great! When can we start?" Brittany exclaimed. Her expression dared Lauren and Jody to comment on her earlier reluctance.

Jody exchanged a look with Lauren, trying not to laugh.

November 26 — early morning — La Gomera
Wow, I was so tired last night I didn't even write in my diary! We were all wiped out from the journey and went to bed early — practically after dinner!

Anyway, I will try to catch up now. I was the first up for breakfast, and now I'm sitting out on the terrace with a cup of hot chocolate — yum! — and a bowl of fresh fruit.

The view here is fabulous. The house is up higher than I realized. I am looking down a big, sloping ravine — what they call a barranca *here. And on either side there are more mountains. The highest peaks are invisible. There's a veil of mist hanging over them. It is totally beautiful!*

Nicole told us that there is a national park at the center of the island that has one of the most ancient forests on earth. It's not like the one we visited in Venezuela. This one is filled with pines and laurels and tree heathers. The center of the island has a completely different "mini-climate" from everywhere else. It's wet there most of the time, but hot, dry, and sunny everywhere else.

Maybe I should do something about the rain forest for my project. Maybe there are some animals that live there. But I can't help being more interested in the animals in the sea . . . If I can't do dolphins, how about whales?

Oops — have to run! Everyone else is almost ready to go!

Their first morning on La Gomera was spent on a beautiful beach, which Mr. Davis told them was the best on the whole island.

"A lot of the beaches here are rocky," he explained. "And in places, the currents are too strong for swimmers. But this beach is as good as any on Tenerife — and much less crowded."

Jody was surprised to see that the beach had black sand. When she stepped onto it, though, she found that it was as soft and fine-grained as the pale golden sands she remembered from the Bahamas.

As Jody settled herself down on the sand she noticed a fruit seller walking along the beach toward them, carrying a load of bananas.

A piercing whistle rang out from a man behind him. The fruit seller stopped, turned around, and whistled back.

The other man whistled again in a complicated series of notes.

The fruit seller nodded, then gave another, different whistle.

"It's like they're talking!" Lauren exclaimed.

"Talking the way dolphins do, by whistling?" Jody asked, puzzled.

"I think you're right," said Nicole thoughtfully. "I've read about a special whistling language used on La Gomera. It's called *silbo*."

"Oh, wow," Lauren exclaimed. "That's really cool! I'd love to find out how it works —" She broke off, then gazed at Nicole. "Hey, could that be my project?"

"Sure, why not?" Nicole agreed. "Why don't you ask him about it right now?"

Lauren hesitated. "What if I can't make myself understood? My Spanish isn't very good."

"I'll help you," Gavin Davis offered. "It'll give me a chance to practice my Spanish." He reached into his jacket pocket and pulled out a tiny cassette recorder. "I always carry this with me in case I have a brilliant idea while I'm away from my computer," he added with a grin. "It's got a blank tape in it. You could use it to record them whistling!"

"Thanks, Mr. Davis," Lauren said, smiling broadly. "That's just perfect!"

Jody watched as Lauren and Mr. Davis went to speak to the man. She was startled to hear another whistle, very close at hand. Turning, she saw that the whistle had come from Hal.

"Rosie," he said in his strange, flat way.

"That's right, Hal," Jody said, smiling at him. "That's

Hal shows me how to whistle. . . .

like the sound Rosie and the other dolphins make. And Lauren talks to them by whistling sometimes. You talked to Rosie that way, too, didn't you?"

The little boy nodded. And then, to her amazement, he answered her smile with one of his own.

November 26 — afternoon
We're in the car, headed for San Sebastian, where Mr. Davis wants to make sure the boat he hired will be ready to take us out whale watching tomorrow.

I need to get started on my own project, especially now that Lauren's got hers! On the ferry, Mario told me that there are about five hundred pilot whales living in these waters — so that's what I'm going to study. And guess what. When I looked up the pilot whale in my marine wildlife guidebook, I found out that it's not really a whale, but a dolphin. Fingers crossed that we see some tomorrow and I can take some pictures!

Jody had expected that they would go directly to the docks near the ferry terminal where they had arrived the day before. But instead, Mr. Davis drove up in front

of a white building with a sign in three languages iden-
tifying it as the Santa Cruz Marine Rehabilitation Center.

"What is this place?" Brittany asked as he parked
the car.

"Why not come inside with me and find out?" he suggested, undoing his seat belt and climbing out.

Jody, Lauren, and Brittany exchanged quizzical
glances, then followed the Davises through the front
door.

A tall, thin man seated behind an untidy desk looked
up as they came into his office. Then he broke into a
smile of delight and jumped up. "Gavin! My good
friend!" he exclaimed, rushing over to fling his arms
around Mr. Davis. He kissed Janet Davis on both
cheeks, then crouched on the floor in front of Hal.
"You must be Hal," he said. "I'm José."

Hal stared at him. In his expressionless voice he said,
"You whale-man?"

"Whale-man?" José's dark eyebrows shot up comi-
cally. He looked at Hal's father. "What have you been
telling him?"

Gavin Davis grinned. "Only that you're coming to sea

45

with us tomorrow to give us a private whale-watching tour. I hope you're not going to turn me into a liar."

"I'm at your service always," José replied, with a little bow. "Now, who are these young ladies?"

Mr. Davis quickly introduced Jody, Brittany, and Lauren. "This is my old friend José Gonzalez," he told them. "We've known each other since college. He's an expert on the wildlife on La Gomera and a few years ago he opened this place, the Santa Cruz Rehab Center."

"What is it for?" Lauren asked. Jody had been wondering the same thing.

"We're a marine wildlife rescue center," José explained. "We try to help any seabirds or marine animals that are found injured or distressed. Sometimes we get called out; other times people bring animals in. We give them whatever help we can and release them back into the wild as quickly as possible." He ran a hand through his unruly brown hair. "But let's not stand here talking — come see for yourselves!"

He led them down a hallway and through a door, into an area that reminded Jody of a row of kennels. In one large cage she saw a seagull huddled in a corner.

"Right now, fortunately, we don't have too many patients," José said. "Last week we were busy cleaning seabirds after they got caught in an oil spill. This gull was the only one too ill to be released right away."

"Is it going to be all right?" Lauren asked anxiously.

José smiled at her. "Yes, it looks like he's going to pull through. Now I'll show you our star patient."

He led the way to a larger enclosure that had a small pond sunk into the concrete floor. Lying in the shallow water was an enormous turtle.

Hal pushed forward curiously.

"It's a sea turtle," José explained. "There are a lot of them in the waters around the Canaries, so we often get them in here. This one had a nasty accident — probably with an outboard motor. He's lost part of a flipper, but he seems to be managing OK. He's much better now than when we found him. We're hoping we can release him next week."

Just then the door swung open behind them.

"*Hola, José*!" called a strangely familiar voice.

"Ah, here comes my number one assistant," José said.

Jody turned to look. She stared as she saw who it

was. "Mario!" she blurted out in surprise as she recognized the boy from the ferry.

The boy looked startled for a moment, then broke into a huge grin as his eyes met hers. "Jody!" he exclaimed. "I didn't think I told you about Santa Cruz. I should have known you'd be interested in seeing it!"

"You didn't tell me," Jody said. "I didn't know anything about it until Mr. Davis brought us here. What are *you* doing here?"

"Mario is a volunteer," José explained. "In fact, he's the best volunteer worker I have! He comes every day after school and most weekends, too. I really don't know what I'd do without him," he concluded, slapping the boy on the shoulder and smiling warmly at him.

Jody was surprised when, instead of smiling back, Mario dropped his gaze to the floor and said nothing. She wondered if he was embarrassed at being praised.

"Well," said José, looking quizzically at the others, "I guess I don't have to introduce you?"

"We met Mario on the ferry yesterday," Mr. Davis explained. "He really hit it off with the girls."

"With Jody, you mean," Brittany put in sharply. "She practically talked his ear off — wouldn't let Lauren or me get near him!"

Brittany's words stung Jody. She couldn't think of a reply.

Mario looked up, seeming surprised. "That's not true," he said quickly. "It's just that when I found out Jody's parents study dolphins for a living, I had to know every detail! I made her tell me everything. So Jody was only being nice to me." He finished with a lopsided smile.

Brittany seemed taken aback. She shrugged. "I was only kidding," she muttered.

Jody gave Mario a quick, grateful smile.

"Why don't you come out with us this afternoon, Mario?" Gavin Davis suggested. "Then maybe you could get to know all of us better."

Mario brightened, then his face fell, and he shook his head. "No, I can't — I'm too busy — I'm sorry."

"Oh, go on," said José. "I think I can manage without you for one day!"

But Mario shook his head. "My parents need me

home early today," he explained. "I only came by to speak to you, José, but — you're busy. I'll come back tomorrow."

"You don't really have to rush off, do you?" José asked. "Stick around for a few more minutes. I've nearly finished the tour — then we can go back to my office, just you and me, OK?"

Mario nodded.

He looked unhappy, Jody thought, and she wondered why.

"I'll show you the dolphin pool," José announced, leading them through another door.

The door led outside to a large, empty concrete pool. Not far beyond the pool area was the sea.

Hal rushed forward to look into the pool. "No water," he muttered.

"That's right, there's no water in it now, because we're not using it," José said. He pointed to the far end of the pool, and Jody noticed that it was connected to a canal that led to the sea, though this was blocked off by a watertight door.

"A few years ago, a small circus got hold of a couple

of dolphins. There were protests about their treatment, and the circus was shut down," José began.

"Good!" Jody exclaimed hotly.

"Yes," José agreed, nodding sympathetically. "However, the dolphins were in a very bad way, and we worried they might die if they were simply released. I volunteered to help rehabilitate them, and a wealthy benefactor paid for the construction of the pool."

From the way he paused and glanced toward Gavin Davis, Jody felt sure she knew who that benefactor had been!

"Within a couple of months, the dolphins were fit and well again," José continued. "Luckily, they hadn't been in captivity long enough to forget how to feed themselves, and we knew they'd been captured in this area, so we were able to release them not far away."

"More dolphins?" asked Hal.

"I think Hal wants to know if you ever get any other dolphins who need looking after here at Santa Cruz," Janet Davis said.

José nodded soberly. "Occasionally, we do get some injured dolphins. Unfortunately, those stories haven't ended so well. Generally, they have been too badly injured for us to treat. And we're not equipped to deal with anything much bigger, so we can't help any of the pilot whales or bigger cetaceans that collide with the ferries."

Jody was horrified. "The ferries run into them?"

Mr. Davis frowned. "Is this something that happens often?"

"Far too often," José told them. "Ever since the high-speed ferries started running between Tenerife and La Gomera, the number of fatal collisions has gone up."

"Can't something be done?" Janet Davis wanted to know.

"The ferry operators could slow down," José replied. "The old-style ferries used to travel at about twenty knots. If the new ferries would slow down to that speed, it would make a big difference."

Jody had been vaguely aware of Brittany fidgeting beside her. Now she saw her turn and walk toward Mario, who was hovering at the edge of the group. But, as Brittany drew near him, Mario abruptly turned and hurried back into the building.

Brittany's shoulders slumped. Then she scowled. "What's wrong with *him*?" she demanded.

"I think what we were talking about was making Mario uncomfortable," José told her.

"You mean because he works on the ferry?" Brittany asked.

"Not only that, it's the fastest ferry of all," Jody added. She frowned in bewilderment. "Why doesn't Mario quit his job? I would. How can he stand to work on a ferry that hurts whales and dolphins?"

"It's not that simple," José said quietly. "Mario's father owns the ferry."

4

November 26 — night
I can't stop thinking about the whales and dolphins being in such danger from the ferries here. Why can't Mario talk to his dad about slowing down his ferry? After all, he says he cares so much about whales and dolphins. He knows how important it is!

Jody paused, gazing down at her diary. She longed to talk to Mario about this idea. If only he hadn't rushed off like that!

She looked across the room. Lauren was tucked in

bed with a book. She looked rather pale, and Jody guessed her arm was aching after their long day. Brittany was sitting in front of the mirror, brushing her hair. Jody told them what she was thinking. "I can't understand why Mario hasn't persuaded his father to slow down his ferry. If he did, maybe the other ferry operators would do the same."

Lauren looked up from her book. "I'm sure Mario's tried," she replied.

Jody shrugged uncertainly. "But if he *has* explained the problem to his father, then why does his ferry still go so fast?"

Brittany set down her hairbrush and turned around to glare at Jody. "Maybe Mario's dad doesn't care what his son wants — or care about hurting animals. Did you ever think of that?"

Before Jody could answer, Brittany went on, "You don't know how lucky you are, Jody. Your parents are *nice*. They listen to you. They care about the same things you care about. It's not like that for everyone, you know."

Jody felt bad for Brittany, whose own mother had

55

dumped her with her father for a year without asking her, without even telling her that's what she was doing. Now her mom was in Paris, engaged to a man Brittany couldn't stand. Jody tried to imagine how tough that must be for Britt, who was right — sometimes Jody did forget how lucky she was!

Lauren got out of bed and walked over to sit next to Brittany. She put her good arm around her and hugged her. For a moment Brittany sat stiffly, then she relaxed and hugged Lauren back.

After a moment Brittany pulled away, blinking rapidly to keep from crying. "I'm OK," she said quickly. "It's just that I know what it's like to have a parent who won't listen to you. Don't kid yourself that Mario can talk his dad into anything."

Jody had the awful feeling that Brittany might be right. She saw from Lauren's expression that she felt the same way. Jody turned back to her diary.

OK, maybe Mario has tried to talk to his dad and his dad didn't listen. But we can't give up! The lives of whales and dolphins are too important. I don't know what we can do, but there must be a way to help. I will talk to Mario about it if we see him again. If we put our heads together, we're bound to come up with something.

They were all up bright and early the next morning for their first whale-watching tour.

The rented boat was an elegant, two-masted schooner called *Rainbow*. The captain, Pablo Torres, was a balding man with a friendly, weather-beaten face. His grown-up son, Pancho, had come along as crew. Neither man spoke much English, but this didn't matter as José would be their guide.

As they sailed out of the harbor, José gave them some whale-watching tips. "You need to look out for the tiniest clues. These waters are full of whales, but the whales tend to stay underwater. If you see a strange-looking wave, or a patch of rough water, that could be a whale's back just breaking through. They may splash with their tails. If you see many birds gathered in one area, that usually means there's lots of fish in the water, and whales and dolphins may be feeding underneath."

Everyone listened carefully. Even Hal was still and silent.

"But one of the best signs," José went on, "is what's called the blow. That's the whale breathing through the blowhole on top of its head. Depending on the size of the whale, the breath can look like a white flash of spray, a little cloud, or even a puff of smoke."

José stopped to draw breath himself, then said, "Now, I know you'll want to shout and point if you see something, but it's very hard to follow somebody's pointing finger, and the whale may be gone before everybody else knows where to look! So we use the clock system. Think of the boat as a big clock with numbers on the face. The bow — the front of the boat — is twelve o'clock. The stern, or back, is six o'clock. Starboard — right side — is three o'clock, and port — left — is nine o'clock."

José paused. "OK, Jody, if I said, 'Whale at seven o'clock,' where would you look?"

Jody thought for a moment, then turned and pointed left and back.

"Bravo," José said, grinning. "OK, everyone: 'Whale at two o'clock.'"

Everyone except Janet Davis turned forward and to the right — she was looking left. The same thing happened on their next try. "Oh, dear, I'm awful at this!" she wailed in dismay. "I just can't remember which side the numbers are supposed to be on!"

Hal gave a little grunt and patted his mother's side. "Hal help Mommy," he said. "See whales."

"Dolphins at four o'clock!" José's voice rang out, and this time it was not a test.

Jody saw a sleek, dark gray creature leap high out of the water and then down again. Three others moved rapidly in and out of the waves. Yes, they were dolphins, but not the bottlenose or Atlantic spotted kinds she was most familiar with. The shape of the head and beak were longer and narrower, and they were darker in color.

José used his binoculars. "Just normal dolphins," he said. "See the hourglass pattern on their sides?"

Jody grabbed for her own binoculars and had a

better look. The dolphins were mostly dark gray, with yellowish flanks fading to a creamy white on their bellies. She noticed a dark V shape just below the dorsal fin on all of them and guessed that was the pattern José had meant.

"What are 'normal dolphins'?" she asked, puzzled by a name she'd never heard.

Taking a peek at the long-beaked common dolphins!

"Oh, that's just what everybody calls them," José replied. "If you want to look them up in a reference book, they're long-beaked common dolphins."

Jody hoped the dolphins would come closer, but they were too busy chasing fish and soon passed out of sight.

As Jody gazed out at the gently swelling sea, hoping to glimpse another leaping dolphin, she suddenly heard Gavin say, "Whale at three o'clock!"

Jody turned to starboard and caught her breath at the magical sight of a whale's blow. It was a delicate, silvery, funnel-shaped cloud that hung above the sea for a few moments before disappearing into the spray.

Then, a few yards away, another blow appeared. Then another. And another. At least a dozen air spouts shot up like a magical forest of clouds. Everyone aboard *Rainbow* gasped in wonder.

"It's a whole pod," José remarked as they sailed closer. "Fifteen, maybe even twenty of them."

As the boat drew nearer, Jody could make out several big black shapes in the water. Only the tops of their smooth heads broke through the surface. Although, at about twenty feet long, these cetaceans were bigger than any dolphin she'd ever met, Jody was surprised to see how much they looked like dolphins. They had dorsal fins and the same body shape. And they didn't seem as big as she'd expected whales to be. . . .

"They look like dolphins," Lauren commented.

"These are short-finned pilot whales," José replied. "But despite the name, Lauren is right — they are actually dolphins."

None of the pilot whales seemed bothered by the approaching boat, and they didn't move away when Pablo and Pancho took in the sails to slow their progress, eventually coming to a halt.

Suddenly, one of the smallest pilot whales reared up out of the water into the air. It faced them, as if it wanted to get a good look at the people on the boat.

Hal gave a shriek of delight. "Hello, whale!"

José chuckled. "Yes, Hal. I think he is saying hello! He's probably the same age as you because the grown-up pilot whale almost never behaves like that. But the young ones are more playful."

"Isn't that behavior called spy-hopping?" Jody asked as the whale sank back down, only to rear up into the air again, headfirst. It looked as if it were balancing up-right on its tail. From this position Jody could see that the pilot whale didn't look quite as much like a dol-phin as she'd first thought. It had a bulbous, rather squared-off head, and lacked the pointed dolphin beak.

"That's right," José agreed. "If you know much about bottlenose and other dolphins, you'll recognize a lot of the pilot whale's behavior." He glanced around at the others and explained, "Despite their size, they are very much like the dolphins Jody's parents are studying. Pi-lot whales dive more deeply than other species in order to get their favorite food, which is squid and oc-topus. They live in groups called pods, which are their families. There can be anywhere between ten and sixty pilot whales in one pod. I think they're the most socia-ble of all the dolphins, because you never see a pilot whale on its own. The group is so important to them that if one gets in trouble the others stay with it."

"I've read something about that," said Gavin Davis, looking thoughtful. "Doesn't that lead to mass strand-ings sometimes — where one whale gets stuck in shal-low water or on a beach, and the others follow it?"

"Yes, sadly, that does happen," José admitted.

Jody was leaning over the side, pressed close against Lauren, Brittany, and Nicole as they all gazed at the massive creatures in the water. The one that had been spy-hopping vanished back below the water. Then they saw that it was leaving the main group, swimming straight toward the *Rainbow*. Seconds later, two other whales also broke away and swam after it.

"They come say hello!" Hal exclaimed.

Jody grinned happily. It certainly looked that way! She was thrilled at the chance to get a closer look at these beautiful creatures.

The one in the lead was much smaller than the two who had followed it. As it came nearer to the boat, Jody saw that it was only slightly bigger than a full-grown male bottlenose, and she wondered if it could be a baby.

Suddenly, the little one launched itself upward, lifting itself almost entirely out of the water before falling back again. As it splashed down, a great spray of water flew up, showering everyone at the railing.

Everyone gasped or yelped at the unexpected dousing. Hal burst into a peal of delighted laughter. After a moment, everyone else started laughing, too.

"I thought whales didn't do that," Gavin Davis said, taking off his glasses to wipe them.

José chuckled. "The adults don't," he said. "Full-grown pilot whales only 'porpoise' when they're traveling really fast. Porpoising means lifting most of the body out of the water," he explained, seeing that Janet Davis was looking puzzled.

"So that one *is* a baby, then," said Jody.

"Young, anyway," José agreed. He pointed down into the clear water where the two larger pilot whales were resting just below the surface, one on either side of the frisky one. "See those two looking after him?"

"Are those the parents?" asked Nicole, leaning over to have a better look.

"Not exactly," José replied. "One of them is the mother, certainly. I'd guess she's the one on the left. The other one is what we call an aunt. She might be the mother's sister, but not always. Females in the same pod always help one another with their calves, and there's usually at least one who is especially close to the baby. She takes over when the mother isn't around."

Jody excitedly turned to Nicole. "Since my report is going to be on the pilot whale, could I film these whales now?" she asked.

"That's a good idea," Nicole agreed, getting the camcorder out of her bag. "It's all set and ready to go," she said. "Just be careful that the baby whale doesn't jump up and grab it out of your hands!"

Jody laughed. "I'll be careful," she promised. She hoped that the mother and aunt wouldn't decide to keep the calf away from these nosy humans by herding it back to the safety of the pod. Fortunately, it seemed that the adults recognized there was no threat from *Rainbow*. To Jody's delight, the young pilot whale continued to perform for the camera, splashing and diving, porpoising and spy-hopping, and all the time squeaking and chattering away. The two adults responded to the calf's noises with their own regular whistles and squeaks.

Finally, though, playtime had to end. The pod was moving again. The two adults shepherded the calf back to join the others.

Jody went on filming as the pilot whales swam away out of sight. She sighed happily, wishing that the rest of her schoolwork was this much fun.

With the excitement over for now, Janet Davis suggested it would be a good time to have lunch. While José helped Pancho and Pablo get the boat under way again, heading for the Tenerife–La Gomera channel, Jody, Brittany, and Lauren set out the large picnic that Diamantina had prepared.

After lunch, the afternoon passed swiftly. Jody was thrilled to catch her first sight of a sperm whale — it was such an immense, awesome creature. She also managed to get a photograph of a solitary Cuvier's beaked whale, coursing swiftly below the surface of the water.

At last the Davises decided it was time to head back to the harbor in San Sebastian. Jody was looking forward to e-mailing her parents all about the whale-watching trip. Leaning over the side, gazing out to sea, Jody noticed what seemed to be a pilot whale all by itself. Surprised by this unusual sight, she fumbled for her binoculars.

"José!" she called as she struggled to bring the shape in the waves into focus. "Look over there — is that a pilot whale on its own?"

"Let's take a look," replied José. He called out directions in Spanish to Pablo, asking him to bring the boat around.

"No, it's not alone — there are two of them," Jody said as she got her binoculars focused. She frowned, feeling uneasy. Only two? And something about them seemed familiar. . . .

"It's an adult pilot whale and a calf," José announced. He sounded worried. "I can't see any sign of the rest of the pod. Could they be diving?"

As he spoke, Jody's eyes narrowed. It looked as though the adult whale was supporting the calf, keeping it above the surface. She seemed to be pushing it toward the boat. There was something odd about the slightly jerky motion. . . . With a jolt of horror, Jody realized that the calf was not swimming. It was injured. She could clearly see deep, fresh cuts in its side — and they were bleeding. The calf was in serious trouble!

5

"That calf is hurt!" Jody cried out as she gazed over the side of the boat at the approaching pilot whales.

There was no doubt about it. As *Rainbow* drew closer, they could all see that the young whale was bleeding from several deep cuts on one side. It seemed to be too weak to swim, because the adult was propping it up with her own body, keeping it from sinking. She was calling, too — a series of anxious squeaks. There was no sign of the rest of the pod. Jody had the feeling the two whales were asking for help.

Jody felt Lauren grip her hand on the railing as she leaned out to look. "Isn't that the calf we saw earlier?" Lauren asked.

Jody had been wondering the very same thing. It did look very familiar. "But there were two adults looking after that calf," she pointed out.

"What happened?" Brittany voiced the question in all their minds.

"Looks to me like some sort of boating accident," José said grimly.

Jody gasped. "A ferry?"

José hesitated, then shook his head. "This *is* the route the ferry takes between Tenerife and La Gomera, and the time's about right, but . . . well, if the calf had been struck by a ferry, I don't think it'd be alive now. On the other hand, if it was hit by a smaller boat, scraped by a propeller or something . . .

"Or maybe it was attacked," José went on. "There are killer whales in these waters, and sharks. Usually the pod is very good at protecting itself. They stick together, and if there's an attack, they put the young and weak members of the group into the middle and defend them. But if a young one strayed a bit too far away, it might get into trouble."

"Where *is* the rest of the pod?" Gavin Davis spoke up. Jody noticed that he was scanning the water with his binoculars.

"These two seem to be all on their own," Nicole pointed out. "Isn't that unusual?"

"Very," José agreed. He sounded tense and unhappy. "Something's wrong."

Jody felt someone pushing against her leg. She looked down and saw that Hal was squirming to get to the railing to see. When Jody saw that his mother had a safe grip on his hand, she moved over to make room for the little boy. He stared down at the pilot whales without speaking. His face was blank. Jody wondered if he understood what was happening.

"Is there some way we can help?" Gavin Davis asked José in a low, urgent voice.

"Could we take it to Santa Cruz?" Janet Davis put in. "A vet could look after it there. . . ."

They all turned anxiously to José, waiting for his answer.

He shook his head, raising his hands in a gesture of helplessness. "How? Transporting a whale isn't easy. Not even a small one like this. Even if we managed to get it on board — well, the shock of being out of the water and separated from its family could do a lot of harm."

"But we have to help!" Jody burst out. "There must be something we can do!"

José's eyes were dark brown and very gentle. He looked directly at Jody. "I know how you feel," he said softly. Then he turned to Gavin Davis. "May I use your phone?" he asked.

"Yes, of course!" Mr. Davis exclaimed, reaching into his jacket pocket for it.

"I'll call Valeria," José told them as he took the phone and began to tap in a number. "She's a vet who's had some experience with marine mammals," he explained. "She was really helpful when we had the dolphins to look after."

When José began speaking rapidly in Spanish, Jody turned her attention back to the whales in the water. Nothing had changed; the adult was still supporting the calf. Looking at it carefully, Jody was convinced that she had seen this pilot whale before, with this same calf. But was this the mother or the aunt? And where was the other adult? Adult and calf seemed to be talking, exchanging high-pitched squeaking sounds. Not for the first time, Jody wished she could understand the language of dolphins.

"Blood," Hal said clearly beside her.

Jody's heart turned over. She could hardly bear to look at the calf's injured side. She felt sick with worry.

"It may not be so bad," Lauren said, her voice soft but determined. "I've seen dolphins get injured before. It's like with us — sometimes you can cut yourself and bleed all over the place and it looks *awful*, but it's not really serious."

Hal turned to stare at Lauren. "Doctor?" he asked.

Lauren nodded. "José is calling the doctor to ask what to do," she explained.

Hal nodded. "Doctor fix whale," he said in his flat, unemotional voice.

Jody hoped with all her might that he was right.

José finished his call and held out the phone to Janet

Davis. "I've asked Valeria to stay on the line," he said. "If one of you could talk to her at this end, you could pass my questions on to her and give me her advice." He began to unbutton his shirt.

"You're not going into the water, are you, José?" Gavin Davis asked.

"Yes, I must. I need to examine the calf," he explained. "I need to assess the extent of the injuries." He paused, then looked at Gavin Davis. "I'll need someone else in the water to help me —"

"I will," said Jody at once.

José looked surprised. He shook his head. "This is a job for an adult, Jody," he said gently. "These are big, wild animals. One of them is in pain, and the adult female will be feeling very protective. She might not want us to come close. I know you're concerned, but dealing with animals is not always straightforward. You'd have to —"

"I *know*," Jody burst out impatiently. Then she bit her lip, realizing she'd been rude. "I'm sorry. It's just that I know a lot about dolphins in the wild. I've even helped a hurt calf before — it had been caught on a fishing line, with a fishhook snagged in its skin. I held it still while my dad dug out the hook."

José nodded, looking thoughtful.

"Jody and Lauren are both used to dolphins," Gavin Davis explained. "I've seen them in action, and I have to admit either girl would do a much better job of helping you than I could!"

"I wish it could be me," Lauren spoke up. "Unfortunately, I'm out of action." She indicated her broken arm. "But Jody's had more experience around wild dolphins than I have, anyway," she added firmly.

"Well," José said slowly. "It sounds like I couldn't have a better assistant than Jody!" He turned to her. "But you must be careful. Stay back until I tell you to come over."

"Now, how long will it take you to get ready?" he went on with a smile, slipping his shoes off.

Jody grinned and peeled off the shorts and T-shirt she was wearing over her swimsuit.

Seeing that José and Jody were getting ready to go into the water, Hal indicated that he wanted to join them and began to make a fuss.

"Not now," Nicole said firmly. "Hal, listen to me. The baby whale is hurt."

"Blood," said Hal, remembering.

"Yes, that's right," Nicole agreed, nodding. "Jody is going to help José try to make the whale better. You can watch with me from the deck, but you must be quiet. If you make too much noise, you might frighten the baby whale, and your friends won't be able to help it."

"Hal be quiet," the little boy promised solemnly.

"There's a good boy," murmured his mother, bending down to give him a hug.

Jody was full of conflicting emotions as she slipped off the side of the boat and followed José into the ocean. There was the thrill of getting so near these magnificent animals, and pride in being able to help José, but she was also deeply worried about the pilot whale calf, and frightened in case José decided that it was too badly injured to survive. What if there was nothing they could do to help it?

The water felt cool and welcoming. Up close, the pilot whales were even bigger than they looked from the boat. Even the baby was bigger than a full-grown bottlenose dolphin. Jody couldn't help feeling nervous as José indicated she could join him and she swam toward them. These pilot whales lived in deeper water than the dolphins she'd met before, and so were less used to meeting people. In addition, the calf was hurt. The adult would be very protective of it. There was no telling how either of them would react. José and Jody only wanted to help, but would the whales know that?

Just ahead of her, José had stopped and was treading water. "OK," he said quietly as she reached him. "We'll take it slow and easy. Stay at a reasonable distance, and don't come forward unless I call. If the whales seem upset by us at all, we'll leave them alone. If I think they're feeling threatened, I'll make this sign —" He held up one finger and jabbed it toward the boat. "If I do that, Jody, you're to head straight back for the *Rainbow* immediately — got it?"

"Yes, José," Jody replied.

He smiled. "OK, then. Slow and easy."

Jody kept back as José swam closer to the pilot whales.

She saw the adult's eye fixed on them, bright and

intelligent. Jody couldn't help feeling that the whale knew they'd come into the water to help.

But what about the calf? Was it even conscious? Jody could see that it was breathing, and every once in a while a shudder rippled through its gray flesh. Was it frightened? It must be in pain. Jody caught her breath in sympathy as she got a better view of the calf's damaged side. Up close, the bloody cuts looked even more horrifying — fresh and painful.

Jody watched as José inspected the cuts and swam around to check on the calf from other angles. He even dove beneath the surface to look at the calf's underside.

Finally, he swam back to her. "A lot of the surface skin has been scraped off," he said quietly. "And I'm sure it's very painful for the poor thing. But the wounds don't look very deep, and as far as I can see, they are clean. I don't think they'd need to be stitched."

This sounded like good news, but José's face was grave.

"Will the calf be all right, then?" Jody asked.

"I don't know," José told her. "I really don't know. I

Swimming with José to the injured calf . . .

think it's in shock. Or there might be internal injuries. Whatever the reason, it's in trouble. The whale isn't swimming, and I didn't see any obvious physical reason for that."

Jody bit her lip anxiously. "What are we going to do?"

"I don't think there *is* anything we can do," he replied. "Not here and now, anyway. I'd feel better if Valeria could have a look at the calf. Come on, let's get back on board. I want to ask her advice."

Jody cast one final look at the two pilot whales and then, tense with worry, swam back to the *Rainbow*.

Pancho had hooked a portable ladder over the side, so they were able to climb back on board without any trouble. Nicole and Lauren were waiting with towels. Jody wrapped herself up gratefully. She'd started to shiver, although it was with emotion rather than cold.

José didn't bother with a towel. He took the phone from Janet Davis immediately and began to speak in rapid Spanish to the vet on the other end of the line. No one else spoke until, finally, José finished his call and passed the phone back to Gavin Davis.

"Well, what's the verdict?" Gavin Davis asked.

José began to dry himself off briskly as he replied. "Valeria can't say whether or not there's been any internal damage. She says we'd need to get it to Santa Cruz and keep it under observation for a couple of days before she could tell, only I'm not sure how we can get there. . . ." His voice trailed off. "If there's nothing except the surface wounds wrong with it, it could recover without needing any help. But the next twenty-four hours will be crucial." He looked grave. "It would be dead already if not for its aunt."

"Why do you say that's its aunt?" asked Lauren. "Isn't she its mother?"

"No, I don't think so," José replied. He slipped his shirt on and began to button it up. "When we saw the three of them together, I thought this one was probably the aunt. She looks a little too old to be a new mother. Besides, it fits in with my theory about what happened."

"Your theory?" Gavin Davis repeated.

José nodded. "I think the injured calf's mother was

81

killed by colliding with a ferry. I'm sure you've noticed how closely the young ones stick to their mothers. I'd guess that the boat just grazed this calf when it killed its mother, but she managed to protect the calf from the worst of it. If it had been hit directly by a ferry, it would never have survived. We'll never know for sure what really happened. Often, with ferry collisions, the bodies of the whales are washed out to sea and never recovered."

Tears sprang to Jody's eyes and she suddenly found it hard to breathe as she imagined the horrible, fatal impact between the mother whale and the speeding ferry.

José went on. "Pilot whales stick together, we know that, so I've been wondering where the rest of the pod might be. I suppose the blow from the ferry might have knocked the mother and calf in one direction, while the pod was traveling in another. Maybe the aunt was already with the mother and calf, and just managed to avoid getting killed herself, or maybe she left the pod to go looking for the missing whales. Once she realized that the calf was hurt, she stuck with it and kept it alive, even though it meant being separated from the rest of the pod."

They were all silent for a few moments, thinking about what José had said.

"So what now?" Jody asked.

"I'm not really sure." José looked uncertain. "You see, we don't have any way of transporting a pilot whale — not even the few miles between here and Santa Cruz."

"But if we could get the calf there, you could look after it, keep it safe?" Janet Davis said.

"Yes, of course," José agreed. "The dolphin pool is not ideal for pilot whales, but for just a few days, while we monitored the calf, it would be OK."

"Then we'll get it there," Gavin Davis said firmly. "There must be people who know how to transport whales — specialists with proper equipment. Let's get on the phone now and organize it. I don't care what it costs — I'll pay for it."

Jody's heart lifted. But then she saw that José, although smiling, was shaking his head. "My generous friend," he said. "This time, money is not the problem. Yes, there are special boats and special equipment to help whales in trouble. But it would take *at least* twenty-four hours to get it here, and it will be dark in less than three. Time, my friend. There is not enough time."

Gavin Davis sighed, his shoulders slumping. "I guess you're right," he said sadly. "I hate to admit it, but —"

Jody interrupted. She'd had an idea. Maybe it was crazy, maybe it wouldn't work, but they had to give it a try. "Maybe we don't have to get it onto the boat," she said urgently. "Maybe . . . maybe we could get the whales to follow us to Santa Cruz!"

6

José joined the girls at the rail and looked down into the water. The pilot whales had stayed nearby. The aunt was still supporting the injured calf. After a moment, José shook his head.

"They won't follow us," he told Jody. "It's true that pilot whales do sometimes follow boats, like dolphins do, but those two aren't in the mood for playing. The calf has been injured. The adult will be concentrating on caring for it. Why should she follow us?"

"Because she needs help!" Jody said urgently. She

looked down at the two creatures, and her heart went out to them. Then she looked back at José, desperate to make him understand. "She's been separated from the rest of the pod. She can't look after the calf on her own. I think she knows we want to help . . . after all, she came up to us in the first place." Jody bit her lip. "Please, can't we at least *try* to lead them to Santa Cruz?"

José was silent for a moment. Then he nodded. "Yes, of course we can try," he agreed. He spoke briefly to the man at the helm, who smiled and nodded vigorously.

"We'll go slowly and try to keep them with us," José explained. "If they fall behind, we can circle back and try to pick them up again."

Jody sighed with relief. "Oh, thank you, José!" she exclaimed.

"But Jody," he cautioned, shaking his head, "this will only work if the whales *want* to follow us. If they don't, there's nothing we can do."

As *Rainbow* moved away slowly under sail, Jody hung over the side, gazing down. Lauren was on one side of her, Brittany on the other. They all watched anxiously and were relieved when the bigger whale began to move, keeping pace with the boat and pushing the calf along, too.

"It's only a few miles to San Sebastian — maybe they will follow us that far," José said thoughtfully. He turned away. "Gavin, may I use your phone again? I'll ask Valeria to head for Santa Cruz right now, and tell Thomas to fill the big pool — just in case!"

"Oh, please keep following, Aunt," Jody murmured after a few minutes had slipped by in silence. "We can help you!"

"Come on, Tía," Brittany said coaxingly.

Jody looked at her in surprise. "Tía?" she repeated.

Brittany flushed self-consciously. "It means 'aunt' in Spanish," she explained.

"It's a great name for her," Lauren said warmly. "It sounds cute."

"Much better than Aunt," Jody agreed, smiling.

Brittany smiled back, looking pleased. "Now we just need a name for the baby," she said.

They watched the pilot whales gliding slowly through the water and thought about it.

"How about Sebastian?" Jody suggested. "Since we're near San Sebastian."

The other two girls looked uncertain. "That's a bit of a mouthful," Lauren pointed out.

"Well, we could call him Seb for short," Jody said.

Brittany nodded, convinced. "Seb and Tía," she said.

"I like it," Lauren agreed. Suddenly, she frowned. "Hey, they're falling behind," she said anxiously.

Jody leaned out over the rail. "Hey, come on, Tía," she called. "Stick with us! Don't give up now!" Dismayed, she saw them falling still farther behind as the boat sailed on. "Oh, no!" she cried. "We're losing them!"

Brittany turned around and called out something in Spanish to the captain. To Jody's relief, he responded by taking in the sails, slowing the boat.

Lauren began to whistle. Jody remembered that this was how Lauren called the dolphins to her at her home in Florida. She sounded uncannily like a dolphin herself.

For a moment, it seemed to have no effect.

Then Tía began to swim toward the boat, pushing Seb along before her.

Lauren continued to whistle. José came to see what was happening.

They all watched in amazement as Tía responded to Lauren's call.

"Pilot whales often swim with groups of dolphins," José told them. "It wouldn't be surprising if they understood each other. . . ." He looked at Lauren curiously. "I wonder what our whistle means to them."

Lauren didn't stop her whistling to comment.

Instead, Brittany spoke for her. "She's saying, 'Follow us. We're friends,' " she suggested shyly.

And, as Tía continued to help Seb to follow the *Rainbow*, while Lauren went on whistling, this did seem to be what Lauren was saying. Tía and Seb were still with the boat when the Santa Cruz Marine Rehabilitation Center came into sight.

A woman dressed in denim jeans, with short, dark auburn hair, was waiting on the rocky shoreline beside the canal that led into the dolphin pool.

"That's Valeria," José said as he waved at her. "I can

see the pool is filled, ready, and waiting for our patient —
if only we can get him into it!"

Jody had been wondering how they would manage
this last tricky part. Now, watching José pull off his
shirt and kick off his shoes, she understood that he
meant to join Tía and Seb in the water.

"Can I come in and help?" she asked.

José nodded. "OK," he agreed. "But remember what I
told you before, and don't get too close. Keep especially clear of their tails. Whales often use their tails de-
fensively — Tía could probably knock you out with a
blow from hers! We don't want to make them feel
trapped. I think it might be best if you swam well
ahead of them, along the channel into the pool — that
might encourage them to follow you."

Jody slipped into the water off the side of the boat
and struck off toward the opening of the canal. She
wanted to look back to see if Tía and Seb were following, but decided it would be better to concentrate on
keeping a steady course toward the canal.

Once she'd entered the waterway, there were no
waves, so the going was easier. As she reached the end

of the canal and swam into the big pool, Jody paused and let herself rest, gently treading water. She turned to look back the way she had come.

For a moment, there was nothing. No sight of anything in the canal. No sound but the gentle lapping of water.

Then she heard a familiar, plaintive, squeaking call.

A moment later, Seb's bulbous head appeared. He shot forward into the pool, pushed from behind by Tía. With a powerful flex of her long, black body, Tía joined

A helping hand up to the surface!

the calf, nudging and supporting him toward the surface.

Happy tears stung Jody's eyes. They'd made it!

November 27 — bedtime
I really didn't want to leave Seb and Tía — but of course they're not alone, they've got each other. And it's probably better if they don't have too many people around them all the time since we want to release them back into the wild as soon as possible. José is going to stay all night at Santa Cruz to keep an eye on them. Valeria agreed with José that Seb's wounds didn't look too bad, but she was worried by his behavior. It seemed all wrong to her. She said that the pain from the cuts shouldn't have stopped him from swimming on his own. She was afraid that he might have been hurt in a way that didn't show — he might be bleeding inside, or he could have been hit on the head and has a concussion. Either of those things would make him slow and sluggish — and might kill him in the next few days.

I guess it was silly of me to think that all we had to do was get Seb to Santa Cruz and he'd be all right.

Still, at least they'll be safe tonight from sharks and killer whales. Tía can get a little rest, too.

But as for me, I feel as if I won't be able to sleep a wink tonight.

Jody did sleep, but she had a restless night. As soon as she woke the next morning, she began to worry about Seb. Was he better or worse? Was he even still alive?

Jody knew she wouldn't be able to think about anything else until she had seen the two pilot whales again. Luckily, everyone else felt the same way. Over a quick breakfast of fresh fruit and warm rolls, Gavin Davis set out the plans for the day. "We'll stop by Santa Cruz first, to check on Tía and Seb," he said. "Then we'll see the sights of San Sebastian."

José met them when they arrived. From the smile on his weary face, Jody knew at once that it was good news.

"The calf is swimming," he said quietly.

"That's great!" Gavin Davis exclaimed warmly.

"Well, it's great news that he's survived the night," José agreed cautiously. "But there's still a long way to go before we can say he's all right. You just missed

Valeria. She came here to check on the calf before going to her clinic."

"What did she say?" Jody asked.

"She was pleased to see he was doing better, but she thinks he looks sluggish. That might be normal after the shock he's had, but it could be a bad sign. She's still worried he might have a concussion," José replied.

"Can she do anything about it?" Jody wanted to know.

José shook his head. "We'll just have to watch and wait," he told them.

"Could we go and say hello to them?" Lauren asked.

"Yes, of course," José agreed. "Follow me."

Nicole kept a firm grip on Hal as they went through the building to the outside pool. "Remember, Hal, this is not a swimming pool for people," she said firmly.

For a moment, Jody thought the pool looked empty. Then, with a soft explosion of breath from her blowhole, Tía's big black head erupted from the water. A moment later, Seb pushed up beside her and swam under and around her body.

Jody winced as she caught sight of his bloody, flayed side. She heard Lauren catch her breath with horror.

"It looks worse than it is," José assured them. "Most of that is just a bad scrape. There's only one deep cut, and even that doesn't need stitches, according to Valeria. With a little luck, that should heal up fine in a week or two. I'm more worried about the problems we *can't* see."

They watched the pilot whales for a few more minutes. Although Seb was swimming by himself, no longer needing to be supported by Tía, he wasn't the active, spunky young whale they'd first seen. The accident had changed him — instead of boldly striking off on his own, he stayed close to Tía. He nuzzled up against her and pressed the length of his body against hers, as if for comfort. And he moved very slowly.

"We should be going," Gavin Davis said at last, breaking the silence.

Jody felt reluctant to leave. "Could we come back later?" she asked.

"Yes!" Hal shouted.

His father looked surprised. "Sure," he said warmly, ruffling Hal's hair. "We'll stop by this afternoon."

"Will Mario be here then?" Jody asked José as they walked away from the pool.

"I'm expecting him. He's here after school most days," José replied, leading them back through the building.

"Good," Jody replied. "I want to talk to him. I'd like to know what his father has to say about this latest accident — killing Seb's mother."

"Jody, we don't know that it was Mario's father's ferry," Gavin Davis pointed out. "We're not even certain that Seb's mother is dead."

"His mother must be dead," Jody replied, shaking her head stubbornly. "I've been reading up about pilot whales, and a mother would *never* abandon her calf. If she has to dive deep to feed, the aunt baby-sits — but the mother comes back right away."

"Jody is right," José replied. "We'll never know how it happened, but I think we can be sure the mother whale is dead. But as to whether it was the speeding ferry —"

"Some kind of boat hurt Seb," Jody interrupted. "It *could* have been his ferry — or one of the others. The ferry operators have to start going slower to stop things like this from happening again! Mario should talk to his father about it."

"You're right, Jody," José said. "But please don't

blame Mario for not trying. I happen to know that he *has* talked to his father about it. Señor Gomez was not pleased with me. He thought I was trying to turn his son against him, as if Mario couldn't think for himself!" José sighed and shook his head.

"What about the other ferry operators?" Gavin Davis asked. "After all, Mario's dad isn't the only one — his is the fastest, but the others are a danger to whales as well."

They had reached the front of the building now and paused beside the door.

"Last year I approached all the ferry operators and tried to convince them to go slower for the sake of the whales," José said. "I explained that it would only mean cutting their speed down by a little, adding maybe another fifteen minutes or so to the journey time. Not one of them would even consider it." He shrugged and finished wearily, "I've given up trying to convince them."

Jody stared at him in dismay. "You can't give up!" she exclaimed. "There's got to be a way to make them slow down — there's just got to be!"

7

Jody could not stop thinking about the whales. Not just Seb and Tía, but all the pilot whales, the bigger whale species, and the dolphins in the Tenerife-La Gomera channel whose lives were being threatened by the speeding ferries.

She trailed after the others through the streets of San Sebastian, hardly noticing where they went as she brooded about the problem. How could they get the ferries to slow down?

"Jody!" Brittany's impatient voice broke into her thoughts.

Jody looked up, blinking. "What?" She found that they were standing in front of a big, square brick tower, and everyone was looking at her.

"Earth to Planet Jody! Honestly, what's wrong with you?" Brittany demanded. "I just asked if you'd film me. I'm not sure Lauren can manage the camcorder with one hand."

"Why do you want to be filmed?" Jody asked.

Brittany rolled her eyes. "For my project, of course! I'm going to be like the reporter giving the news about Christopher Columbus — you know, like if they'd had TV reporters in those days."

"Christopher Columbus?" Jody repeated, baffled.

"Oh, Jody! Weren't you listening to Nicole at all?"

Jody bit her lip and gave Nicole an apologetic look. "Sorry . . . I was thinking about something else," she confessed.

Nicole smiled at her. "I can guess what! I just said Columbus was one of La Gomera's most famous visitors of all time. San Sebastian was the last port of call for the *Nina*, the *Pinta*, and the *Santa Maria* before they set sail across the Atlantic."

"So I can film the house where he stayed and the well where he got the water he took to the Americas and all that," Brittany said. She turned and pointed up at the imposing old brick-and-stone tower. "And this is where Columbus's girlfriend lived! She was called Beatriz de Bobadilla."

"This is the Torre del Conde," Nicole explained. "It's one of the oldest buildings in the islands, dating back to 1447. It's a museum now, so why don't we go inside and have a look?"

"And try to pay attention this time, Jody," Brittany murmured.

Jody shrugged and followed the others inside.

After the museum, they visited Casa de Colon — Columbus's house — and the Gothic church where Columbus had prayed for God's blessing for his historic voyage of 1492. Jody pointed the camcorder while Brittany played reporter. Nicole carried a clipboard and helpfully jotted down details about each scene.

"There should just be time to buy a few souvenirs before lunch," Janet Davis said as they turned down a street full of small shops.

"Oops, I know which shop I'm going into," said Nicole as Hal suddenly dashed through a doorway. Thrusting her clipboard into Jody's hands, she chased after the little boy. Jody saw that he'd been attracted by a big plastic dolphin hanging in the window.

Going inside, Jody saw that the shop specialized in whale- and dolphin-themed gifts. As well as plastic, rubber, glass, and cuddly toy dolphins and whales, there were ceramic bowls, plates, and mugs painted with leaping dolphins, T-shirts printed with stunning photographs of whales, posters, postcards. . . .

Jody picked up a postcard featuring a pod of pilot whales. Close beside her, a girl's voice said, "We saw them today!"

Jody turned and saw a blond girl who looked about seven or eight. "Do you mean pilot whales?"

The girl nodded enthusiastically. "Yes! And some dolphins! We saw them from the ferry. Daddy says we can go on a whale-watching cruise. I saw loads of them advertised in the harbor."

"We'll go tomorrow, Jenna," said a bald man with a camera slung around his neck. He smiled at the girl. "Remember, we're only on La Gomera for the day. But there are even more whale tours leaving from Tenerife."

"Daddy, can I buy some of these postcards?" Jenna asked.

"Sure, go ahead," her father replied. Coming closer, he inspected the postcards. "Nice pictures," he commented. "I'll bet none of mine comes out that well."

"You can try again when we go back," Jenna said. "We might see the whales again. Maybe they'll come closer to the ferry next time."

"Just hope they don't get *too* close," Jody said darkly.

Jenna and her father looked at Jody in surprise. "Why not?" Jenna asked. "They're friendly, aren't they? They wouldn't try to hurt us?"

"They won't hurt us — but we can hurt *them*," Jody said. Suddenly, the image of the injured calf came vividly into her mind. She remembered Seb bleeding and shocked in the water, and burst out, "It's not safe for the whales out there anymore. The ferries travel too fast. The whales can't get out of the way in time. And when they're hit, they usually die."

Jenna's eyes were huge. "How awful!" She gasped, horrified.

"It certainly is," her father agreed. "Does it happen very often? Isn't there anything the ferry operators can do about it?"

"Yes," Jody told him. "Yes to both — it does happen often, and it could happen much less often if only the ferries would slow down a little bit. If they would just cut their speed to twenty knots, it would make a huge difference!"

"Then they should do it," the man said. He put his hand out. "Here, I'll sign your petition."

Jody stared at him in surprise. She looked down at the clipboard in her hand and then back at him and shook her head. "This isn't . . . there isn't a petition."

"There isn't? Well, there should be," the man said firmly. "Do you know, I read that nearly a million visitors came to Tenerife to watch whales during the last year. If that many people really care about whales, they wouldn't mind if it took a little longer to cross between La Gomera and Tenerife — not if it would help the whales!"

Looking thoughtful, he went on. "The ferry operators would certainly slow down if they thought that was what their customers wanted. That's probably why they speed up in the first place! After all, a business has to please its customers. No matter what they think about the whales, if a million customers asked them to slow down, they surely would."

The man looked at his watch, then turned to his daughter. "Come on, Jenna, pick out your cards and I'll pay for them. We've got a ferry to catch." He looked back at Jody. "Thank you for telling us about this. I'll write a letter to the ferry operator myself."

"Oh, would you? That's great! Thank you," Jody said warmly.

"But I'm just one person," her new ally reminded her. "To make a difference, they need to hear from hundreds — even thousands of people. Take my advice and get a petition started."

Jody nodded vigorously. "I will," she agreed. She was suddenly full of excitement and hope.

Over lunch in a harborside fish restaurant, Jody told the others about her new plan.

They all agreed it sounded like a good idea. "Most

visitors to La Gomera aren't in a hurry," Mr. Davis pointed out. "People come here for a vacation because they want to relax and enjoy nature."

"That's right," Mrs. Davis agreed. "And they're not commuters! Who's going to mind if the journey from Tenerife takes fifteen minutes longer than it does now? That just means fifteen minutes more to enjoy the sun, the fresh air, the birds, the sight of basking whales and leaping dolphins!"

"So you think a petition would be a good idea?" Jody asked hopefully. "And the ferry operators would respond?"

Gavin Davis hesitated. "Well, I don't know for sure how the ferry operators would respond, but it's worth a try. Presentation could be key. You don't want it to sound like a demand." He paused to think again, and then his face lit up. "I know!" he exclaimed. "Instead of a petition, why not a survey?"

Jody frowned. "What do you mean?"

He explained, "Why not ask visitors what they want? Which is more important to them — getting across to La Gomera quickly, or having a more relaxed journey with the chance to observe whales and dolphins? Would they support a 'whale-friendly' ferry service?"

Nicole spoke up. "That would make a good project for you, Jody."

Jody nodded slowly, her mind buzzing.

"And if the results are what you hoped for, you could present your findings to the local tourist board and the ferry operators," Gavin Davis concluded. He grinned. "Businesses pay good money for market surveys to tell them how to improve their services, you know. And you're doing it for free!"

"I'm not doing it for their sake," Jody objected. "I just want to save the whales!"

Gavin Davis smiled at her sympathetically. "Then your best chance is to convince the ferry operators that what's good for the whales is *also* good for them," he said firmly.

After lunch, they drove back to the Santa Cruz Marine Rehabilitation Center. Jody couldn't wait to talk to Mario about the new plan.

But Mario wasn't there. By the time they'd had a brief visit with Seb and Tía it was past four o'clock, and Mario still hadn't shown up.

"Come on, time to go," Gavin Davis said briskly, steering Hal toward the door. "We've got lots more to do today."

"Oh, can't we stay a little longer?" Jody asked. "I really wanted to talk to Mario about the visitors' survey. Or — could I stay? And you could pick me up later?"

But Mr. Davis shook his head reluctantly. "That would be difficult. We weren't planning on coming back in this direction."

Suddenly, José spoke up. "I could drive Jody back to your house this evening," he said.

"We can't ask you to do that," Mr. Davis objected. "It's out of your way. . . ."

"You're not asking, I'm offering," José pointed out. "It's no problem."

"Why don't you come to dinner as well?" Janet Davis suggested with a warm smile.

"Thank you," José replied. "I'd enjoy that very much. I've heard Diamantina is one of the best cooks on the island!"

Soon after the others had left Santa Cruz, Mario arrived. "How is the calf?" he asked anxiously as he rushed in.

"He's looking much better," José replied. "A little more lively, although he still hasn't eaten anything. Why don't you go with Jody and see for yourself?" he suggested. "You can help me clean out the turtle pen afterward."

Mario looked unhappy. To Jody's surprise, he shook his head. "No, I'm sorry, I can't stay. . . . I shouldn't really be here at all," he mumbled. "But . . . I had to see him again."

José looked faintly puzzled, but he spoke gently. "That's all right, Mario. If you've got schoolwork, your studies have to come first, before working here."

Mario stared at his feet and muttered, "I can't work here anymore."

"Oh, Mario, why not?" Jody cried.

Mario looked at her. "My father said so," he explained

miserably. "Now that the winter tourist season has started, he needs me to help out on the ferries every weekend. And after school, he says if I have time left over from my studies he will find other things for me to do."

Jody thought this sounded very unfair. But José said calmly, "I understand, Mario. December and January are a very busy time on the island. Your father needs

Mario breaks some bad news.

you more than I do. In the spring when things calm down, you can come back."

Mario shook his head. "No," he said. "You don't understand. My father won't let me. He says he's tired of me wasting my time helping out for free at Santa Cruz when there are better things to do with my time. José, I'm very sorry, but I can't come here again."

8

Jody could hardly believe it. How could Mario's father be so cruel to forbid him to help out at Santa Cruz?

"May I please go and see the pilot whales now?" Mario asked. "I can't stay long."

"Sure, sure, go ahead," José said. He still looked stunned by Mario's news.

Jody hurried down the hall after Mario and caught up with him outside, standing at the edge of the pool. Beneath the water, Seb was nestling close to Tía. Becoming aware of the visitors, the calf broke away from his aunt and swam quickly to the surface, poking his whole head out of the water in order to breathe and take a good look at them at the same time.

The sight of the calf being his old curious, energetic self brought a smile to Mario's solemn face. "Hey there, Sebastian," he said softly. "How are you doing?"

Seb ducked his head under the water and flipped his body over. His broad, flat tail poked up out of the water for a moment, then slapped down hard, spraying water into the air.

Jody and Mario first gasped and then whooped with delighted laughter as they were splashed.

"I guess he is feeling better, after all!" Mario exclaimed.

"It's so great to see him playing again!" Jody agreed. The cuts and grazes on the calf's side still looked sore to her, but they obviously didn't bother Seb too much.

Jody and Mario stood in silence for a few moments, watching the calf swimming around. But he soon tired and returned to nuzzle close to Tía.

Mario sighed. "I guess I'd better go," he said.

"Wait," Jody said. "I need to talk to you."

He stopped and looked at her curiously.

Jody had been meaning to explain her plan and ask him to help her with the survey. But now she wondered if that was wise. What if it made his father angry? She didn't want to make things even worse for Mario.

"Well, what is it?" Mario asked when she didn't speak.

Jody replied with the first thing that came into her head. "Why won't your father let you help out at Santa Cruz? Is he punishing you for something?"

Mario shook his head. "No! No, Jody, it's not like that! My father isn't cruel — he really wants the best for me," he said earnestly. "And he needs my help now. Maybe it's different where you come from, but ours is a family business. Everybody helps out."

"I do understand," Jody said. "But even if he needs you to help in the busy season, what about the rest of the time? Can't you do anything else but work for your dad?"

Mario sighed. "Oh, yes. My father is thinking about my future," he explained. "Jody, I'm fifteen. My father is right when he says I should start planning for my career, maybe get a part-time job that would help me get ahead."

"What sort of career do you want?" Jody asked.

Mario looked away from her, at the pilot whales resting in the pool. "I'd like to work with animals," he said quietly. "I'd like that more than anything. Sometimes I think I'd like to study them — especially to study the whales. Like your parents study dolphins! Or maybe I could be a vet."

Jody stared at him, her mouth open. "But — this is the *perfect* place for you to get practice in working with animals!" she exclaimed. "Your father must know that!"

Mario hunched his shoulders. "He doesn't know," he muttered.

"He doesn't know what?" Jody demanded. She stared at him, wide-eyed. "Haven't you told him what you want to do?"

"I tried to. . . ." Mario sighed unhappily. "He doesn't really listen to me. He thinks animals are just a hobby, and that they couldn't be a career."

"What does he think you're going to do, then?" Jody asked.

Mario shrugged. "Go into business. I'm good at languages and math. He wants me to study business." He sounded resigned to this fate.

Jody shook her head. "Mario, you have to talk to your father! Tell him what you want — what's important to *you*. He can't make all the decisions and run your life for you!"

Mario looked at her unhappily, shaking his head. "You don't know my father," he said simply. "Anyway, I have to go now. Good-bye, Jody. Maybe I'll see you again on the ferry."

"Mario, wait!" Jody cried. She gestured toward the pilot whales in the water. "Won't you come back to say good-bye to Seb and Tía when they're released?"

Mario gazed at the dark bodies resting in the pool just beneath the surface, and a wistful smile appeared on his face. "Yes, of course," he said softly. "I'll come back one more time."

After Mario had gone, José came out with buckets of fresh squid and small fish. "Feeding time!" he called out.

"Can I help?" Jody asked eagerly.

He smiled at her. "Yes — maybe you can tempt the calf to eat."

José watched closely as Jody tossed a squid into the pool. The calf darted forward and caught it in his mouth. "Good, Seb's got his appetite back," José murmured. "He didn't eat yesterday, and that worried me."

Jody noticed that Tía seemed to be holding back, giving Seb a chance to feed first. But it was soon obvious that Seb didn't need any help. After a few moments, Tía also began to go after the food. The two pilot whales bumped and jostled each other in a friendly way as they fed.

"Valeria's planning to come by and examine Seb first thing on Friday morning," José said. "If he keeps improving at this rate, I'm pretty sure she'll recommend releasing them on Friday."

"I'd like to be here to see them go," Jody said.

José smiled at her. "Don't worry. I know how much Seb means to you. It would be nice to have all his friends here to say good-bye."

When the squid was finished, Jody followed José as he took the empty bucket away. "I'm sure Mario's dad would let him go on working here if he knew how important it was to him," Jody began.

"You may be right," José agreed. Stopping beside the big outdoor sink, he began to wash his hands.

"You could tell him," Jody suggested. "If you talked to Mario's dad and told him how Mario feels . . ." She trailed off and frowned because José was shaking his head.

"Why not?" she asked. "Why won't you talk to him?"

José finished washing this hands and moved to one side so Jody could use the sink. As he dried his hands on a towel hanging nearby, he explained, "This is between Mario and his father. I can't interfere. Mario is growing up. He'll have to decide what to do with his life. His father has one idea, Mario has another. If it's truly important to him, Mario will have to learn to stand up for what he wants."

Handing the towel to Jody, he added gently, "I can't fight Mario's battles for him, and neither can you. This is something he'll have to sort out for himself."

The next morning, everyone set off for San Sebastian in the car. Once there, they arranged when and where they would meet up and separated into groups.

Nicole had offered to go with Brittany and Lauren to work on Brittany's project about Christopher Columbus. Gavin took Hal off to explore the seashore.

Janet Davis volunteered to help Jody with her survey. "I speak German pretty well, so I could explain it to German tourists, while you talk to the English speakers," Mrs. Davis suggested.

"Thanks," Jody said. But she sighed, adding, "I guess we'll just have to miss out on all the Spanish visitors. . . . I wish Mario were here to help!"

"I think Jody has a crush on a certain boy," Brittany remarked with a smirk.

Jody felt her face get hot. "I do not!" she said angrily. "I like him as a friend, that's all! I only meant it would be good to have someone who spoke Spanish to help us."

Nicole stepped in swiftly. "We're meeting up at lunchtime, right? By then Brittany's film should be all wrapped up, so we can all help out with the survey in the afternoon. Lauren can help you with the English tourists, I'll take the Spanish speakers — and Brittany can help me, since her Spanish is so good."

This praise from Nicole made Brittany smile and

flush self-consciously. She forgot all about teasing Jody and agreed to help with the survey later.

When the others had gone, Jody and Mrs. Davis stationed themselves at the ferry terminal and waited for the next ferry to arrive. They each carried a clipboard with a neatly typed copy of the survey and a pen to record the answers. They also had stacks of flyers to hand out. Jody had composed it the evening before, and Gavin Davis had printed out hundreds of copies on the computer at the villa. It was in English on one side, and in Spanish on the other. Briefly, it explained the plight of the whales and dolphins, the danger they were in from the fast ferries, and how much safer they would be if the ferries would slow down to a whale-friendly speed of twenty knots. Jody felt she'd done a very good job of writing it.

While they were waiting for the ferry to arrive from Tenerife, Jody wandered along the harbor front and approached some people waiting in line to board a boat for a whale-watching tour. Jody was pleased to find that most of the tourists seemed interested and happy to answer a few questions.

As Jody checked the boxes to record their answers —
yes, they were concerned about the safety of whales
and dolphins; no, they wouldn't object to a slightly
longer ferry journey; yes, they would choose a ferry
that advertised itself as being whale-friendly — her
spirits lifted. But not all of the ferry passengers who
were soon flooding the dock were as responsive as the
whale watchers. Many did not want to answer her
questions or read the flyer. Despite La Gomera's laid-

Down by the harbor with my clipboard!

back reputation, some visitors were clearly in a hurry to "do" the island before rushing back to Tenerife on the fastest boat available.

By lunchtime, when the others joined them at the agreed meeting place, Jody had sixty replies to her survey. Janet Davis had collected fifty-four. And the overwhelming majority were in favor of going slow to save the whales.

After a delicious picnic lunch of cold chicken, cheese, fruit, pastries, and other treats provided by Diamantina, Gavin Davis suggested a quick visit to Santa Cruz. "Hal wants to see Seb and Tía again," he explained. He smiled at his son, obviously delighted by the way the boy had come out of his shell on this vacation.

"Great!" said Lauren.

Jody felt torn. She hated to pass up any chance to see the two pilot whales, but this morning had showed her how long it would take to get a decent-sized survey. This vacation was rushing by too fast! "I'd like to," she said. "But the survey . . ."

"We won't stay long at the center," Mr. Davis said.

Nicole patted Jody's shoulder. "How about if Janet and I keep the survey going while you're at Santa Cruz?" she suggested. "You should be back by the time the next ferry gets in."

"I'll stay and help," Brittany volunteered. She had clearly taken a liking to Hal's nanny.

Jody smiled with relief. "Thanks," she said warmly as she scrambled to her feet.

At Santa Cruz they were met by a serious-looking José.

"I've had some news," he told them quietly. Then he looked down at Hal and spoke more brightly. "Why don't you run and tell Seb and Tía that we're coming?"

Hal started to dash away, but his father restrained him. "Hang on a minute, son," he said.

"I'll go with him," Lauren volunteered. Jody guessed both Lauren and Hal's father were remembering how much he had loved to get into the water with the dolphins at CETA.

"Thank you, Lauren," Gavin Davis replied, smiling at her.

As soon as Lauren had led Hal out of earshot, José

told Gavin Davis and Jody the news. "The body of a female pilot whale has been found washed up on a beach," he said quietly. "It sounds like Seb's mother. And from the injuries, it does appear that she was killed by a collision with a large, fast boat, like one of the ferries."

Jody caught her breath. Tears pricked her eyes. Although they'd all been sure that Seb's mother was dead, they hadn't known the grim details. Now her death was all too horribly real.

"The body is being sent to the veterinary college at Tenerife for examination," José told them. "It could provide valuable information about impact injuries. We never see most of the bodies of whales that are killed in accidents — usually they are swept out to sea and just disappear."

Gavin Davis said, "Maybe you should send details of this whale's death to the ferry companies, along with your survey, Jody. It might have an impact by making the danger more real to them."

Jody nodded slowly, thinking about it. "And pictures of Seb, with his injuries," she added. "We can point out that he's lucky to be alive after his close encounter with the ferry that orphaned him."

"It would be good if Seb's mother didn't die in vain," José said. "If her death meant that other whales would be saved —"

Suddenly, the doors banged open as Hal came charging through. The little boy looked excited as he beckoned to them. "Whales come!" he shouted. "Come see, come see!"

9

Jody ran after Hal, closely followed by José and Mr.
Davis.

When they got outside, Jody saw Seb and Tía still in
the pool, looking much as they had the day before.
One thing was very different: This time, they weren't
keeping quiet. Both pilot whales were giving high-
pitched cries. Jody had heard them call to each other
before, but never both at the same time, or quite so
loudly or steadily.

Lauren was smiling broadly and pointing out to sea.

"They're calling their friends," Lauren explained. "Look! The pod is here!"

Jody followed Lauren's pointing finger. Something was moving out there in the water . . . dark, gleaming bodies . . . was it a group of dolphins? Then she saw the unmistakable shape of tail fins rising into the air and slapping down hard against the water, sending up a fan of spray. It was that distinctive whale behavior known as lob-tailing.

As Jody watched in silent wonder, she heard the pod respond to the cries of Seb and Tía. The faintly eerie sound of their voices drifted inland, making her shiver.

"There must be twenty of them at least!" Gavin Davis said softly.

"Seb family!" Hal cried. A rare smile lit his face. "Seb and Tía not lonely no more."

November 29 — before dinner
Phew, what a day! Between us, we managed to collect answers from another two hundred and eighty people this afternoon. Nearly all of them are in favor of a slower, whale-friendly ferry.

If only we could go on like this for another week, we'd have a great argument to present to the ferry operators. But we don't have much more time — only tomorrow, in fact. We leave first thing Saturday morning.

Valeria is going to examine Seb tomorrow. If she says he is well enough, José will release the whales in the afternoon. He said he would wait until after school so that Mario could be there, too. Seeing Seb and Tía released would be the perfect end to our vacation!

My tummy's rumbling, my mouth is watering, and I can smell something delicious coming from the kitchen. Got to go check it out!

As Jody entered the big living room where the others were relaxing before dinner, Gavin Davis was just finishing a phone call. His face was serious. "That was José," he said.

"I hope nothing is wrong," said his wife.

"The whales are fine," said Mr. Davis, seeing they were all watching him. "But Valeria has had to rush over to El Hierro to deal with some veterinary emergency. She won't have a chance to look at Seb before Saturday."

127

Jody's heart sank as she understood what this meant. "But that's after we're gone," she said heavily.

Mr. Davis nodded. "I'm afraid so. It's a pity, since you've been involved from the start. We'll phone or e-mail you with the good news right away, though I know it's not the same as being here."

"I wish we could stay longer," Lauren said wistfully. "Not just for Seb and Tía, but if we had another week — or even a few more days — we could get more people to sign our survey. It could make all the difference."

"I can't believe we've got to go so soon," Brittany moaned. "We've hardly done *anything*."

"We'd love to have you stay another week," said Janet Davis. "The time has really flown. You know, we've taken this villa for a whole month. . . ." She looked questioningly at her husband.

Mr. Davis nodded enthusiastically. "If your parents agree, I'm sure we could change your flights to a later day."

"That would be *great*," Lauren shouted. Brittany nodded, looking excited.

Jody sighed. She knew Brittany wouldn't like what she had to say any more than she did herself, but there was no point pretending. "It might be OK for Lauren," she said. "But there's no way our folks will let us stay any longer. They've got a schedule to keep. They won't want to stick around Caracas past Saturday."

"*Dolphin Dreamer*'s heading for Bonaire and Curaçao next — am I right?" Gavin Davis asked.

Jody nodded. She remembered her mother had mentioned scuba diving off Bonaire.

"Well, I've been to Curaçao," Mr. Davis explained. "And as I recall, it's no great distance to sail from there to Caracas." His eyes crinkled as he smiled kindly at Jody. "Maybe your folks wouldn't mind picking you girls up from the Caracas airport after they've been to Bonaire and Curaçao, but before they head off to the Panama Canal."

"We could at least ask," Brittany pointed out, and although she still hardly dared to hope, Jody had to agree.

"It's lunchtime in Florida," Gavin Davis calculated,

glancing at his watch. "That might be a good time to get a hold of your parents, Lauren." He handed her his cell phone.

Lauren got through right away and spoke excitedly to her mother. After a little while, she handed the phone back to Mr. Davis. "She wants to talk to you."

"Hi, Alice. Yes, that's right. It's no trouble at all! We'd really like for them to stay. . . . Lauren is just wonderful with Hal. It's been such a treat to have her here, we're dreading having to say good-bye. . . ." He paused, listening, then said, "OK, then, not a whole week — how about if we aim to get her back on Tuesday? Great! I'll call you back later to confirm when I've checked the flight times."

He handed the phone back to Lauren so she could say good-bye. When she'd finished her call, she handed the phone to Jody. "Your turn," she said, holding up a hand to show her crossed fingers. Brittany held up hers, too. She knew her fate was linked to Jody's.

Jody quickly keyed in the number of her parents' phone. There was a pause, then a recorded message that made her heart sink. She sighed and looked around

Trying to get through to Mom and Dad . . .

at the others. "I couldn't get through. They must have their phone switched off," she explained.

Janet Davis came over and patted her on the shoulder. "Try again later," she said. "It's time for dinner now."

Jody gave her a weak smile and went with the others into the dining room, where Diamantina had outdone herself with another magnificent spread.

But Jody had lost her appetite.

November 29 – after dinner
Oh, where are they?

I tried calling three more times, but still can't get through!

The only thing I can think of is that they're out sailing, with the phone switched off. Maybe they're not even going to return to shore until it's time to pick us up on Saturday.

There's no hope. I might as well face it — I'll have to go home without knowing if Seb will be OK, and without getting this survey done properly. Lauren has promised that she'll spend all her extra time working on it with Nicole, so that's something. . . .

Tears blurred her vision, and Jody had to stop writing. She tried to think positively. Whether or not she was here, Seb would be released when he was well enough. And at least she'd managed to get the survey started. She knew she could count on Mr. Davis to send the results to the ferry operators.

132

Just then, there was a knock on the bedroom door. Janet Davis looked in. "There's an e-mail for you, Jody. Come and see!" she said urgently.

Heart pounding, Jody hurried after her.

Dearest Jody,

It's been one minor disaster after another around here. The latest was when I (that's right — NOT one of the twins, not even poor old Dr. Taylor, but good old Dad!) dropped our phone into the deep blue sea! If you've been trying to call us, don't worry. We're all OK and will be getting a new phone tomorrow, I hope.

Also, we are still waiting on a part for the boat. The boatyard here wasn't as well-equipped as Harry thought it would be — they had to send away for some things, and one is still in the mail. It looks like we'll be tied up in Caracas at least until the middle of next week.

We just got an e-mail from Alice and Jerry saying that Lauren would be staying on in La Gomera until Tuesday. There was also one from Gavin Davis explaining why it's so important for you and Brittany to stay for at least a few more days. To put you out of your misery, I'll say right now that this is fine with me, your mother, and Harry. Enjoy yourselves!

Fingers crossed, by the time you're back on Tuesday or Wednesday, the repairs will be finished, Dolphin Dreamer will be shipshape, we'll have our new phone, and will be ready to set sail again!

Lots of love,

Dad

Jody gave a great yell of excitement. She jumped up and punched the air. All at once she felt convinced that everything would go her way from now on.

Saturday morning dawned gray and wet, the first rainy day of the vacation.

But the weather could not dampen Jody's spirits. Today, they were going to Santa Cruz to be on hand when Valeria examined Seb. If she agreed he was well enough, the two pilot whales would be set free.

Jody piled the results of her survey into the briefcase that Gavin Davis had lent her. She thought about what she was going to say to Valeria. José had suggested that the vet might be able to give her some photographs of the dead pilot whale as an example of the damage a speeding boat could do. "Just in case people aren't convinced the ferries need to slow down," José had said. "After all, a picture's supposed to be worth a thousand words."

But when they reached Santa Cruz, they found José alone in his office doing some paperwork. As soon as he saw them, he jumped up and hastily cleared stacks of files off a couple of chairs.

"Why don't you sit down?" he suggested. "Valeria isn't here yet, but she phoned to say she was on her way."

"Hal go see Seb?" the little boy suddenly piped up, tugging at Nicole's hand.

José smiled down at Hal. "Yes, of course. Go right ahead. You can all go, if you don't mind a little rain," he added.

"I'm sure the whales don't mind it," said Nicole as Hal dragged her away.

Jody, Lauren, and Brittany hurried after them. As soon as they came out of the building, Jody could hear the squeaks, whistles, and creaking noises made by Seb and Tía. From out at sea, fainter but still audible, the rest of the pod was calling.

Jody looked at the two familiar dark shapes in the rain-dimpled water and hoped Seb would poke his head up to say hello to her.

The rain was coming down harder now. "It's pouring! We'll get soaked!" Brittany exclaimed.

But even though she was getting steadily wetter, Jody was in no hurry to leave. She glanced down at Seb, then, using her hand to shield her eyes against the rain, stared out to sea where the other pilot whales had been waiting patiently for the past two days. Although Jody felt terribly sad about the death of Seb's mother, it was comforting to know that he was not alone.

"Come on," said Nicole, touching her arm. "Let's get in out of the rain!"

With one last, fond look, Jody left the poolside.

Inside, they found Mario had arrived. His eyes lit up when he saw Jody. "I thought I had missed you!" he exclaimed.

"No, we're getting to stay for a few more days," Brittany told him with a beaming smile.

"Really? That's wonderful news!" Mario said.

"Yes. Best of all, I'll get to finish my survey," Jody added.

"What is this survey?" asked Mario.

"I'll show you." Jody fished into the briefcase for a copy. Handing it to him, she explained quickly what she was trying to do.

To her astonishment, after a quick glance at it, Mario turned pale. "How could you do this, Jody?" he asked, staring at her in disbelief. "Are you trying to put my family out of business? Trying to get everyone to stop using our ferry service?"

Jody felt dismayed. "No, of course not!" she exclaimed. "*All* the ferries go too fast! If you read the whole thing, you'll see! I'm not singling out your father's company — look, at the end I give the addresses of all the ferry companies so that people can write to ask them to slow down. It's for the sake of the whales and dolphins — I thought you cared about them."

Mario nodded, biting his lip. "Yes, of course I agree the ferries should go more slowly. But making a big protest is not the way to persuade people to change!" He looked utterly miserable.

Jody felt terrible. Somehow, she had thought that Mario would understand what she was trying to do. "It's not a protest, it's a survey," she insisted. "They're very different things."

Mario did not look convinced.

Desperately, Jody turned to Gavin Davis. "Can you explain it to him, Mr. Davis?"

"I'll try." Setting his glasses on his nose, Gavin Davis turned his attention to Mario. "Speed isn't the only selling point for a ferry," he said. "There could be others. If Jody's survey shows that, say, eighty percent of passengers would be happier for the trip to take longer in order to protect the whales, a smart businessman might decide to lower his speed, to appeal to that eighty percent. If it worked, and the whale-friendly ferry got more customers than the speedier ferries did, well . . . pretty soon all the ferries would be competing with one another to see which could be the whales' best friend!"

Mario nodded. "I see your point." He began to smile. "If it worked, it would be good for business *and* good for the whales!"

"Absolutely!" Gavin Davis agreed.

Suddenly, Mario's grin froze as a loud, angry voice split the air.

They all turned to look. A dark-haired man stood scowling in the doorway, glaring at Mario. "So, this is how you show respect for your father!" he boomed.

10

Mario's father burst into the room. "I might have known I'd find you here!" he shouted at his son. "I thought I made it clear — you have no time for volunteer work!"

Jody looked at Mario. He seemed to have shrunk into himself and stood staring down at his shoes.

"Well, what do you have to say for yourself?" his father demanded.

Mario shrugged helplessly. He seemed unable to speak.

"I won't stand for disobedience!" his father roared.

Jody couldn't bear it. But before she could think of what to say, José stepped in.

"Rafael, please," he began. "Mario didn't disobey you. He already told me that he wouldn't be able to work at Santa Cruz any longer. He's not here today to work — I invited him to come say good-bye to some friends."

Rafael Gomez looked puzzled, but he seemed to relax a little.

"Why don't you have a cup of coffee?" José suggested. "I'd like to introduce you to my friends."

"Well . . ." Rafael Gomez nodded gruffly. He glanced at his son. "I suppose we could stay for a few minutes. Thank you, José."

"Great!" José said warmly. He glanced toward the door. Jody saw that a car was pulling into the parking lot. "Ah, it looks like the vet has arrived," he observed. José put his hand on Jody's shoulder and said, "This is Jody McGrath. She has come all the way from America to visit La Gomera. She and Mario met on the ferry crossing, I understand. Jody, this is Mario's father, Rafael Gomez. Perhaps you could introduce him to the others while I go and speak to Valeria?"

"Yes, of course," Jody agreed, and quickly introduced Mario's father to everyone else.

"I am surprised," Señor Gomez commented as he shook hands with Gavin Davis. "I had expected only local people to come to the marine center." He looked friendly and interested, and much more like his son now that he had calmed down. "What made you choose to come here?" he asked curiously.

Gavin Davis answered promptly. "The same thing that attracted us to La Gomera in the first place — the wildlife. Especially the sea life."

"Whales!" Hal piped up, to everyone's astonishment.

"That's right!" Janet Davis exclaimed, bending down to hug her little boy. "We love the whales most of all!"

Rafael Gomez looked surprised. "Whales? Surely whales are too big for this center?" He looked at Mario. "I thought you said it was mostly turtles and birds here?"

Mario nodded. "Mostly," he murmured.

His father waited for more, then shrugged impatiently and turned back to Gavin Davis.

"Santa Cruz wouldn't normally deal with anything as

large as a whale," Gavin Davis agreed. "But this was a special case — an injured pilot whale calf."

"Who is hopefully going home today," said a new voice.

Jody looked around and saw Valeria beckoning to her. She left the others and went over to the vet, who handed her a stiff white envelope.

"Here are the photos you wanted," Valeria said in her heavily accented English. "Seb's mother. Not a pretty sight. And there's a copy of my report on the cause of her death."

"Thanks, Valeria, that's really kind of you," Jody said. She wasn't looking forward to seeing the pictures of the dead pilot whale, but if it made people understand how dangerous fast boats could be, the tragedy might not have been in vain.

"I'm going to check on Seb now," Valeria said.

"Can I come and help?" Jody asked eagerly.

Valeria shook her head gently. "No, better not. I'm sorry, Jody. José will help me, and I think it is less stressful for the whales if there aren't too many people around. Afterward, you can all come outside."

Jody was disappointed, but she understood.

Valeria winked at her. "See you later," she said as she went out with José.

Jody looked around. Mario was standing on his own at the edge of the room. She caught his eye and beckoned him over. "Valeria gave me some pictures of Seb's mother," she told him. "Do you want to look at them with me? They won't be nice."

Mario nodded. "I know," he said quietly. "I've seen what happens when a boat hits a pilot whale."

Jody had just pulled the pictures out of the envelope when an angry shout from across the room made her look up. To her surprise, she saw Mario's father, his handsome face once more contorted in anger — only this time, it was directed at *her*.

"You!" he shouted furiously. "Are you the one I've heard about, the girl going around the port saying bad things about my ferry?" He was clutching something in his hand. With a sinking feeling, Jody realized it was her survey questionnaire.

Rafael Gomez stalked across the room, waving the piece of paper furiously. "You are not a friend to my son!"

he raged. "Don't you know that ferry is my family's liveli-hood? If you put me out of business, what do you think will happen to Mario? He can forget about going to college then. If I starve, he starves, too. You are so concerned about these precious whales, but you don't care what happens to people — not even your friend Mario!"

Alarmed, Jody flinched away from him. She shook her head. "No," she began. "I didn't —"

"Leave her alone!" Mario said. His voice was unexpectedly clear and firm. "Jody's my friend," he went on. "She's not trying to put us out of business — she doesn't want to hurt us at all, only to help the whales."

Rafael Gomez looked startled. He seemed too taken aback by his son's interruption to reply. His silence seemed to give Mario the courage to go on.

"Jody's been doing some market research," he explained. "And it could help us. She's been asking the ferry customers what they want. Do they think it is more important to go fast, or more important to slow down to give the whales a chance? She isn't telling them not to use our business."

Señor Gomez frowned. "Whales again! They can learn

to get out of the way. They can swim underwater, they can dive," he said impatiently.

"No!" Mario shouted, cutting his father off. "We go too fast! All the ferries do now. The poor whales can't get out of the way in time! Look, this is what happens!" As he spoke, he thrust the photograph of the dead pilot whale under his father's nose.

"That's Seb's mother," Mario explained, his voice urgent. "She was struck by a ferry and killed. She never had a chance. Now her calf is an orphan. He was injured, too, and he could have died very easily. Come and see what the ferry did to him!" Grasping his father's hand, Mario tugged him toward the door.

Jody hurried after them out to the pool. Everyone else followed.

Outside, the rain had stopped, although the sky was still overcast and the air felt heavy and damp. Valeria and José looked up in surprise as they crouched at the edge of the pool.

"There, look!" Mario said, pointing at Seb. The calf's injured side could be clearly seen, just below the surface of the water. To Jody, who had seen it when the

146

wounds were fresh and still bleeding, Seb looked much better. But to someone seeing the pilot whale for the first time, the injuries looked horrific. She heard Señor Gomez draw in his breath suddenly, shocked.

"A fast ferry did that!" Mario told his father. "It killed his mother, and it nearly killed him."

"Will he be all right?" Señor Gomez asked. He was still frowning, but now he spoke with concern, not anger.

"Yes," said José. "Luckily we found him in time, and luckily he had his tía with him to look after him and keep him from drowning."

"Drowning?" Señor Gomez echoed, looking puzzled. "How does a fish drown in the sea?"

"They're not fish, Papa," Mario said softly. "Whales and dolphins are mammals like us. They need to breathe air. They have a blowhole at the top of their head — that's why they need to come to the surface. Pilot whales can stay underwater without air for nearly two hours, but then they have to come up and spend at least ten minutes breathing again."

Rafael Gomez stared at him. "How do you know so much about it?" he asked.

Mario shrugged. "I read, I listen, I watch them. . . ." He took a deep breath. "This is what I want to do with my life, Papa. I want to study animals, especially whales and dolphins. I want to learn things about them that nobody else knows. And if I can, I want to do something to help them," he finished.

Mario's father was looking at his son as if seeing him for the first time. Then he looked at the pilot whales in the pool. "It's hard," he said, shaking his head. "I had no idea boats could do that kind of damage." He shrugged. "Would it really save their lives if the ferries cut their speed?"

Jody nodded vigorously. "Research has proven that speed makes a major difference," she said.

Señor Gomez sighed again. "Well, it must be right to slow down," he said. "But I'm afraid we'll lose business if we do. . . ."

"Not if you make your new, slower speed a selling point," Gavin Davis put in.

"Do you think so?" Señor Gomez asked him. He still sounded very uncertain.

"I'm sure of it," Mr. Davis replied firmly. "Just think

about why my family and I came to La Gomera. We came to see your amazing wildlife. And all these visitors that Jody has talked to — they love the whales, too. If you're the first to promote your ferry as whale-friendly, you'll be overrun with customers!"

"And once they see how successful you are, the other ferry operators will slow down as well," Jody said eagerly.

Señor Gomez was quiet for a moment, looking thoughtful. "Maybe you're right," he said slowly. "Only last week a passenger said to me that the ocean was so beautiful, he wished he could have spent twice as long on the crossing! On vacation, most people are not in a hurry." He was silent again, then seemed to come to a decision and turned briskly to his son. "I'll make a deal with you, Mario," he said. "Maybe we could try slowing down and advertise ourselves as the whale-friendly way to travel, but I'll need your help."

"How?" Mario asked cautiously.

"You'll have to explain to the passengers about the whales and dolphins and other sea animals they might see during the crossing. That is to be your job — at least during the vacation season," Rafael Gomez concluded.

A brilliant smile lit up Mario's face. "Papa! I would love to do that! There's nothing I'd like better!" he exclaimed.

Jody sighed with relief.

"Well, we've got some good news here," Valeria called from the poolside.

"How's your patient?" Gavin Davis asked.

"Much better," Valeria replied. "All he needed was the chance to rest somewhere safe. His side will probably be sore for a few more weeks — but he's young and healthy. Once he's back home with his family he should be just fine."

"So it's time to say good-bye to Seb and Tía," José announced as he went to open the barrier that separated the pool from the ocean.

Jody gazed down at the two pilot whales. She knew that Valeria and José were right, and that it was time for them to go, but she couldn't help feeling sad at the thought of saying good-bye forever. . . .

"See you soon!" Hal called suddenly, as if he'd read Jody's mind.

"That's right, sweetie," his mother said, putting her arm around him. "We'll see Seb and Tía again another day. We'll be on our boat, and they'll be out in the ocean where they belong!"

Tía seemed to understand what was going on as soon as the channel was open. She began to nudge Seb toward it, letting out a stream of gurgles, creaks, and little mewing sounds.

Jody thought she could hear a faint reply, almost like an echo, from the pod waiting out at sea.

She watched in silence as the two pilot whales left the pool, gliding along the channel with a single flick of their muscular tails, and emerged into the sea.

Then they dived below the surface in perfect unison. Two tails reared into the air. A sudden shift of sunlight glittered on their dark, wet skin for a moment before they vanished. Jody looked up at the clearing sky.

The vast dazzling arc of a perfect rainbow stretched

Seb and Tía following the rainbow!

out of the clouds. The far end seemed to plunge into the gray water. Jody felt happy tears come as she watched Seb and Tía swim steadily toward the end of the rainbow, where their pod waited for them.

You will find lots more about dolphins on these web sites:

The Whale and Dolphin Conservation Society
www.wdcs.org

International Dolphin Watch
www.idw.org

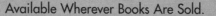